Moonlight, Magic, and Murder

LAGUNA BAY MIDLIFE WITCH
COZY MYSTERY BOOK 3

Moonlight, Magic, and Murder

LAGUNA BAY MIDLIFE WITCH
COZY MYSTERY BOOK 3

DEANNA DRAKE

Fine Skylark Media
California

Fine Skylark Media
P.O. Box 1505
Lake Forest, California 92630

Moonlight, Magic, and Murcer
Laguna Bay Midlife Witch Cozy Mystery Book 3

ISBN: 978-1-957691-05-3

Cover Design by Mariah Sinclair

Thank you for supporting indie authors! Your purchase helps keep the magic alive in Laguna Bay and Citrus Grove.

If you enjoy this book and want others to discover Boo, Kheppy, Rebecca, Aneksi, and all the cats who secretly run the universe (at least in our humble opinion), please encourage friends to buy their own copy rather than sharing this file.

Piracy hurts small creators, and your support means the world.

With whiskers, warmth, and gratitude,

DeAnna Drake

Contents

About the Book

Moonlight, Magic, and Murder

Laguna Bay Midlife Witch Cozy Mystery
Book 3
by DeAnna Drake

When a welcome party ends in murder, midlife witch Boo Boudreaux and her talking cat are on the case—because nothing ruins a family reunion like a body in the backyard.

Boo was braced for tension when her formidable ex-mother-in-law swept into Laguna Bay, putting a damper on Boo's long-overdue reunion with her estranged daughter, Lila. Awkward hugs? Absolutely. Passive-aggressive comments? Guaranteed.

Murder? Not on the guest list.

Evangeline Duval isn't just a difficult relative. She's a high-ranking New Orleans supernatural elder with strong opinions about Laguna Bay's magical leadership. One bad report from her could strip the town of its charter and shatter the safe haven Boo has fought hard to protect.

So when Evangeline collapses mid-celebration, whispers of poison, old grudges, and council infighting spread faster than gossip at the local hair salon. And before long, suspicion starts pointing straight at Boo's own household.

With her sharp-tongued talking cat Kheppy, her fiercely loyal sister Delphine, and longtime friend Merle Foster by her side, Boo must untangle old loyalties, hidden guilt, and dangerous politics before fear tears her community apart.

Moonlight, Magic, and Murder is Book Three in the Laguna Bay Midlife Witch Cozy Mystery series—a charming paranormal cozy packed with:

- A determined midlife witch sleuth
- A magical small-town council
- A clever talking feline sidekick
- Found family
- Clean, cozy suspense

Letter from Boo

Hey there, friend—

Name's Boo Boudreaux. And no, I wasn't born with that name—I picked it for myself when I was seven, after declaring Halloween the best day of the year and deciding I'd never answer to anything else again. Turns out, nobody in Laguna Bay was brave enough to argue with a girl holding a plastic scythe and a sugar high.

These days, I run the Halloween Boo-tique, a little year-round shop filled with spooky delights, vintage décor, and the occasional magical oddity I swear I didn't mean to stock. I share my home (and my headaches) with my younger sister, Delphine, who knows her way around a cauldron better than most, and with Khepeset—who prefers to go by Kheppy—an ancient talking cat who once lounged in Cleopatra's palace and now sleeps on my clean laundry.

I used to read tarot cards. Was pretty good at it, too. But I don't do that anymore. And no, I'd rather not talk about why.

What I will tell you is that Laguna Bay might look like your average coastal town—but that's just the cover.

We're a haven for folks with… well, let's call them extraordinary complications. And while I don't consider myself the magical type anymore, Del and I help keep the town's protection spells running smoothly through the Laguna Bay Horticultural Society. It's mostly garden witches and strong tea, but it does the job.

In *Moonlight, Magic, and Murder*, what should've been a simple welcome party for my ex-mother-in-law turns into a nightmare when she collapses in my backyard before finishing her tea. One minute I'm trying to keep the peace, and the next I'm untangling a murder that hits far too close to home—while juggling old wounds, new suspicions, and a town full of secrets that were never meant to see the light of day.

So pull up a chair, pour yourself a cup of something warm, and settle in.

We've got mysteries to solve, relationships to mend, and—of course—an opinionated cat who's never far away.

Welcome to Laguna Bay.

Warily yours,

Boo Boudreaux

WELCOME TO

LAGUNA BAY

Chapter 1

Spilling Tea

No one else seemed willing to say it, so I did.

I shot up from my folding chair so fast my tea sloshed over the rim of my insulated mug and splattered across the concrete. "We can talk about everyone's Thanksgiving plans later. Right now, we need to decide what to do about Evangeline Duval."

Because Evangeline wasn't just my ex-mother-in-law. She was a supernatural council elder from New Orleans with a nasty habit of stirring up trouble for sanctuaries she didn't like.

And lately, she'd turned her sights on Laguna Bay.

If that wasn't bad enough, in less than twenty-four hours, she'd also be my house guest.

"I know it's a busy week," I added, forcing my voice to steady. "But we have to figure this out tonight. I have a shop to run in the morning, and at some point, I need to get some sleep."

Khepeset—my feline companion, better known as Kheppy—lifted her head from my sister's lap.

"Boo," she said calmly, "it's nearly one a.m., so technically it already is the morning."

Her whiskers twitched as she nudged Delphine's hand, clearly expecting to be stroked.

I sipped my chamomile tea so my frustration wouldn't slip out. "I realize that," I said as the soothing liquid worked its magic. "My point is, we need to come up with a plan because I don't trust that woman."

"Don't be so melodramatic," Cornelia Sloane said, her glossy red lips twisting into the frown that seemed to be her default expression these days. The publisher of the local newspaper and I had never been friendly, but recently our relationship had turned downright frigid. I wanted to ignore her, but since she was our council elder representing local vampires—even if she was the only one of her kind who ever attended our Midnight Council meetings—I couldn't risk alienating her.

Another dilemma to add to the pile.

A gust of cool ocean air rushed into the room as the back door opened. Every head turned to see Merle Foster enter, his soft blue eyes crinkled at the edges as he tipped his cowboy hat. "Sorry I'm late, folks. A motorist required some roadside help."

I'd been wondering what was keeping him. When we'd met for lunch at Beachside Café, I was still reeling from the early-morning call from my daughter, Lila, asking—carefully—if I'd mind if her grandmother tagged along on her upcoming visit.

After nearly a decade of not seeing Lila, she had to know I'd agree to anything. That realization settled heavy in my chest. I couldn't help wondering what had prompted the request. She knew how I felt about Evangeline—and how Evangeline felt about me.

Merle was one of the few people who knew our complicated family history. He'd promised to attend tonight's meeting for moral support. Even with Kheppy, my sister, and the rest of the garden witches around me, I'd felt his absence. Seeing his smiling face now was more reassuring than it probably should have been.

As that rosy glow settled in, a five-foot-nothing slip of a woman in a red sweater and jeans pushed past him, her long blond hair swaying behind her. "Did you already tell them how you rescued me? I'd still be stuck on Legion Street, waiting for a tow truck, if it weren't for you."

I recognized the sassy spitfire instantly—Claire Greenwood. She could see animal ghosts and ran a pet cemetery on the edge of town. Anyone in the supernatural community could attend these meetings, and Claire hadn't missed one since moving to our coastal corner of Southern California a few years ago.

"Just a flat tire," Merle said modestly. "Wasn't too difficult."

"For you, maybe," Claire said. Her smile lingered a second too long, or maybe I was imagining it.

"Do you mind shutting the door?" I groused.

Merle's frown told me he'd caught the edge in my tone. I rubbed my arms and gave an exaggerated shiver, hoping he'd blame it on the draft—even though I was wearing my L.A. Dodgers hoodie, which paired surprisingly well with the blue I'd recently dyed my hair. I'd picked the vibrant color on a whim to cover the gray, and kept it because, well, it suited me.

"Don't be jealous," Delphine whispered, pretending to fuss with a loose thread on her sleeve.

"Who's..." I didn't finish the question. It wasn't Claire. Not really. I'd set the record straight later. Right now, we had to figure out what to do about my ex-monster-in-law because I suspected her visit had more to do with her vendetta against our town than her desire for a family reunion. That's why we had to handle her carefully.

Exactly how to do that was still unclear.

"My gut tells me Evangeline is up to something," I said. "She doesn't like how we run things. She's made no secret of it. Honestly, I'm afraid she's only coming to collect evidence to use against us with the High Council. If she can persuade them to audit us, we'd probably fail. They might even revoke our charter."

"They wouldn't do that, would they?" Claire asked, picking up one of the shortbread cookies Delphine had set out on the snack table. "The community wouldn't survive."

Finally, they were waking up to the reality of what was at stake.

Howard Collins, Laguna Bay Hardware's owner and council elder for the witches and psychics contingent, rubbed his sleepy eyes. "I've heard rumors that some of her complaints are getting traction with a few of the High Council directors."

That earned a round of grumbles.

"Rumors she started, no doubt," said Willa Wendell, my oldest and wisest friend among our circle of garden witches. She rarely spoke during these meetings, so her words resonated all the more now, at least with me.

"It makes sense," Cornelia said. "We haven't sent anyone to the annual gathering in years. It's a miracle they haven't shut us down already."

"It's a bit unreasonable," Delphine said, bristling, which for her meant tightening her lips and straightening the royal blue cardigan she'd crocheted for herself last winter. "Air travel is difficult for some of us."

Neal Glory, the merfolk's representative on the council, as well as one of the most popular hairstylists in town, lifted a hand. "Hey, I fly commercial just fine."

"I wasn't talking about you, dear," Delphine said. "I was talking about—"

"We don't have to out everyone's..." I glanced around the room. "Situation. We all know we've let things slide."

"Come to think of it," Neal muttered, "we never updated the registry of supernatural abilities like they asked for last year. Do you think that could trigger an audit?"

The way Howard and Cornelia stared at the floor and gave half-hearted shrugs didn't inspire confidence.

Laguna Bay had always been the stray cat of sanctuaries—independent, scrappy, and chronically late with its paperwork. I'd had a taste of stricter living in New Orleans before Lila was born, and while I wouldn't blame it entirely for the end of my short-lived marriage, it certainly hadn't helped.

Claire settled into an empty folding chair and faced me. "What does Lila say about it?"

I rubbed my temple. The beginnings of a headache pulsed behind my eyes.

When Lila had called before breakfast, her voice brittle across the miles, my heart had tried to climb right out of my chest. I hadn't seen my daughter in person for far too long. Years of polite calls and letters that never bridged the gap. I'd hoped our reunion would repair that breach and bring us closer together.

Instead, it would now come with Evangeline Duval attached like an anvil.

"She didn't say much," I said. "She didn't need to."

My ex-mother-in-law was a big reason why I'd divorced her son, Luc, and fled New Orleans to return to Laguna Bay when Lila was only a toddler. I'd let Evangeline convince me that leaving my daughter behind was in Lila's best interest—a decision I'd regretted almost instantly and every day since.

A cheerful chime rang out from the leaders' table.

Neal and Cornelia glared at Howard.

"Phones are supposed to be turned off during meetings," Cornelia scolded.

A red-faced Howard fished out his device and tapped the screen to turn it off. Whatever he saw there turned his pink cheeks deathly white. "It's a message from the High Council's secretary. 'Checking in. Let's schedule a chat.'"

"Funny how that comes the same day Evangeline decides to visit," I muttered. Too convenient to be a coincidence.

"What's the big deal?" Jemma asked. Still in her forties, she was the newest addition to our garden witches—closer to Lila's age than the rest of us. "We're not hurting anyone."

Willa patted her arm. "That's not the point. It's about control. They love their rules and their paperwork—and we're not exactly great with either." She cast a pointed look at our local leaders: Cornelia, Howard, and Neal.

"We've always operated on trust," Cornelia said coolly. "Apparently that's no longer sufficient."

"In my defense, the forms are extensive," Howard said.

"They ask so many questions," Neal added, smoothing the gel-slicked side of his platinum fade.

Delphine cleared her throat. "I'm not trying to be a downer, but I heard the Williamsburg sanctuary lost its charter after Evangeline reported its leaders to the High Council for getting sloppy with their supernatural talents registry. When it shut down, some of the residents had to go into hiding."

"That's just gossip," Neal said. "Isn't it?"

No one answered. I hadn't heard about it, but I wouldn't put it past Evangeline.

The room suddenly felt smaller. The fluorescent lights overhead buzzed like a wasps' nest.

As far as supernatural talents went, mine had always been murky at best.

I used to read cards and tell fortunes, but I gave that up years ago. Now I putter around my year-round Halloween shop and help my sister and our gardening group keep the community's protection spells up to date.

Sometimes people assume Kheppy is my familiar, but that's not our relationship at all. I look after her, just as my mother did before me, and Lila will after me. Or perhaps the honor would pass to my granddaughter, Luna.

Either way, it wasn't something I had the mental energy to consider at the moment.

"Are you sure your grandmother wouldn't prefer to stay at a hotel?" I'd suggested when Lila called. "She might be more comfortable. I'll pay for it."

As if the cost would matter to Evangeline. She had more money than some countries. But I would have paid anything to get my daughter away from that ball and chain, even for a few nights.

"It'll be fine, Mom," she'd said. "Grandmama says she wants to see how... you're doing."

That pause spoke volumes.

Sitting in the harsh light of Howard's back room, I felt that familiar mix of guilt and stubbornness rising in my chest. Fine. Let her see the life I had built for myself. My home. My shop. My community. Maybe I didn't always follow the rules, or at least her rules, but I'd done well for myself.

"Let's talk specifics," Merle said, sliding his big frame into a too-small chair beside me.

I raised a hand to interrupt. "Before we get to that, should we discuss whether to include the werewolves?"

The local pack members had kept to themselves for years, but recently seemed to have a change of heart.

Not everyone was ready to welcome them back into the fold, however.

Merle glanced around. "Since none of them bothered to show up tonight, I say no."

He wasn't a fan of werewolves in general, so that wasn't a surprise.

"It's not that we don't want to include them," Howard said, "but they aren't here, and we need to move quickly."

That seemed to be the consensus, but Willa hesitated.

"If Evangeline is looking for shortcomings, excluding them might raise questions," she said.

No one else seemed to agree, so the party planning moved forward. Without werewolves.

"Whatever we do," Merle said, "we need to make it big. We need to make her feel welcome."

"Like an honored guest," Delphine said.

"Exactly," he said. "But where? We don't have a lot of options."

"Beachside Café?" Willa suggested.

"A public place means glamours, wards, and a lot of explaining if anything goes wrong," Neal said. "We'd have to shut the café down, and that could draw unwanted attention."

"What about here?" Claire suggested, glancing around.

Howard paled. "I'd rather not. This place is my livelihood. I don't want to risk it."

I sighed. "We can do it at our house. The backyard cleans up nicely. Remember when we hosted my granddaughter's graduation party a few years ago? Also, it's private, warded, and we can control who comes and goes."

Delphine hesitated. "But Boo..."

"I haven't forgotten about our neighbor," I said. "We'll figure something out. We've hidden stranger things from her than a cranky old witch."

The scene came together in my mind: lanterns in the avocado tree, big round tables scattered across the yard, and Evangeline's razor-sharp gaze sweeping my yard like a code inspector searching for violations.

My stomach twisted.

Kheppy stepped onto my lap, a warm, familiar weight. She kneaded my thigh, her claws politely sheathed.

"There's still time to back out," she said. "You can tell Lila you'd prefer Evangeline did not come."

I stroked the sleek line of her back. "As tempting as that is, I couldn't do that to Lila. You didn't hear her, Khep. There was something in her voice. I couldn't say no. Evangeline Duval is coming, whether I like it or not."

And the truth was, I didn't care. I was going to see my daughter, and I would put up with fifty Evangelines for the chance to spend time with Lila.

Howard pushed back his chair and stood. "We have a plan. Boo and Delphine will host the party, but we'll all pitch in. We need a united front. Also, before she gets here, everyone double-check your paperwork, protections, and anything else that might get us into trouble. If that woman is here looking for problems, let's not give her any ammunition."

"And if she's here to stir up trouble?" Willa asked in a small voice.

The room went silent. I could feel my heartbeat in my fingertips.

Cornelia broke the silence. "Then we smile, we welcome her, and we show her a good time. Let's just hope we do a better job of it than Williamsburg did."

I swallowed hard. The idea of Laguna Bay losing its status as a sanctuary for supernaturals, leaving all of us exposed to whoever—or whatever—preyed on people like us, left me breathless.

Delphine's hand found mine and squeezed. "We're not Williamsburg," she whispered.

"No," I agreed.

But as I glanced around the cramped back room—at the witches, merfolk, mediums, and assorted supernaturals who called Laguna Bay home—I couldn't shake the feeling that we were about to be judged by someone who didn't know the first thing about us.

Tomorrow night, she'd be sitting in my backyard. And for the first time in years, I felt like the girl who had fled New Orleans—unsure, unsettled, and completely unprepared.

Chapter 2

Broken Teacup

Big Sunday night dinners were a Boudreaux tradition—but tonight's welcome party had taken on a life of its own.

The backyard buzzed with nervous energy. Folding tables lined the flagstone path beneath twinkle lights like soldiers awaiting inspection, and I was the frazzled general trying to whip them into shape.

Inside and out, it was all hands on deck. Tablecloths were wrangled into submission, lights were stretched from the porch to the avocado tree, and centerpieces took shape under Jemma's careful eye—even if she looked like she would have rather been anywhere else.

Considering Evangeline's reputation and the trouble she'd already caused, who could blame her?

"Oh, come on," I muttered, giving the last tablecloth a final tug.

Kheppy, of course, chose that moment to point out a table I'd missed.

"I was getting to it," I said.

"You were not," she purred.

"Just making sure you were paying attention."

She glared at me. "I don't think so."

We both knew she was right.

I grabbed another cloth and fixed it before she could gloat any further.

By the time I made my way back toward the house, Sissy was juggling decorations, and the smell of sugar and butter told me the cooks in the kitchen had the dessert situation well underway.

"Del's scrubbing an old tea set," Sissy added as I met her at the door.

Of course she was.

When we'd planned the menu with Evangeline in mind, one thing had stood out from my time in New Orleans: the woman always wanted her daily tea served in fine bone china like she were the Queen of England.

Delphine had apparently pulled our mother's heirloom set out of storage for the occasion.

"How are you holding up with everything?" I asked Sissy.

She gave a small shrug. "I'm still getting used to the idea of being half-werewolf. But it's not all bad."

Before I could ask her to elaborate, Kheppy hopped onto the table beside me, leaving dusty paw prints on my clean cloth. "Boo, when do you plan to visit the neighbor?"

I'd almost forgotten about the woman in the Airstream—the one who considered binoculars a fashion accessory.

If she started paying attention tonight, we were in trouble.

I needed to get to her before she got nosy.

I made it as far as the side gate when I realized that I should take a peace offering with me. I headed inside to see if Jemma had any extra flowers for a bouquet.

As expected, I found Delphine at the kitchen sink, rinsing and wiping Mama's tea set.

"How are things going outside?" she asked, glancing up from her task.

"I was about to head next door," I announced, "but I thought I should take something with me."

Delphine shook her head. "No need. I already took care of it."

I stopped. "You did?"

"I went earlier with a plate of shortbread and a carafe of special tea." Her tone was casual. Too casual.

Suspicion prickled. "How special?"

"Heavy on the chamomile." She smiled sweetly. "With a touch of slumber charm. She'll wake up tomorrow feeling like she had the best sleep of her life."

I sighed and considered confiscating my sister's spell book. "You shouldn't have done that." I hated shortcuts, but I was also secretly grateful.

I stepped around the kitchen table, where Willa and Opal were helping Sissy's mom, Beth, chop and peel apples, to see if Jemma needed help in the living room. She still looked out of sorts as she sat knee-deep in flowers at the coffee table, trimming leaves and stems.

"How's it going out there?" she asked, pushing back a strand of brunette hair that had slipped loose from the clip holding it off her neck. "Ready for the centerpieces yet? I'm working on the last one."

I glanced at the bundle in her hands, then at the arrangements lined up on every surface around her. A dozen, maybe more.

"These are beautiful," I said. "You missed your calling."

She scoffed softly. "I tried the florist thing once. Didn't work out."

Delphine came up beside me. "They are lovely. Are you sure you don't need help?"

Jemma glanced around at her bouquets and shook her head. "I'm fine. I have enough left over to decorate the buffet table, if you want."

A buzz from my phone interrupted us. It was Merle.

Baggage claimed. Heading to the truck. See you soon.

My stomach flipped.

"They're on their way," I told the room.

Delphine rubbed my arm. "It'll be all right," she said. "Remember to expect the best, not the worst."

"Sure," I said, forcing a smile I didn't feel.

For the next thirty minutes, everyone ran around, getting the finishing touches into place and clearing the mess.

I tried to help Jemma clean up, but I was having a hard time keeping my eyes off the window. Thankfully, she took charge, scooping up floral trimmings and shoving leftover blooms into trash bags with brisk, efficient motions.

When Merle's truck rumbled up the drive, she slipped out the back to dump the bags into the trash bins.

Thank goodness for friends, because I was a nervous wreck by the time he lumbered up the pathway, rolling two massive suitcases piled high with smaller bags.

Lila stepped down from the passenger seat and paused, like she wasn't sure what to do with her hands. I hadn't known what to expect after all these years—whether I'd see a stranger or someone I recognized. Now firmly in her forties, she looked composed in her navy coat, the late-afternoon light catching the faint lines at the corners of her eyes and the careful set of her shoulders. Her cinnamon-brown hair fell neatly past her collarbone, framing a face more defined than I remembered—yet there, in the tilt of her head and the guarded way she scanned the yard, I could still see a glimpse of my little girl.

When she stepped forward, slowly, her hug was brief and a little stiff. She felt solid in my arms, undeniably a woman, and still—impossibly—my child.

"It's good to see you, sweetheart," I said, tightening my arms just a little longer than she did. "Luna wanted to be here, too, but she couldn't get away from the bakery."

"She texted me," Lila said quickly, her smile polite but restrained as she pulled back. "It's okay. There'll be time to catch up."

A throat cleared behind her.

Lila stiffened, as if she'd forgotten she wasn't alone. She hurried back to the truck, to the woman still sitting in the back seat. "Sorry, Grandmama. Let me help you."

My daughter opened the rear door, offering a helping hand so Evangeline could ease herself out. At eighty-five, she moved with care—slower than I remembered, but with purpose. Her black hair had gone silver, and it was tucked into an elegant chignon, with tiny curls framing deep-set eyes that missed nothing. Dark lipstick sharpened her slender lips, and her impeccably tailored coat fell perfectly into place. One leather-gloved hand lay on my daughter's arm, deliberate as she stepped down.

I had to hand it to her. Evangeline Duval didn't simply arrive. She arrived in style.

"Mom," Lila said quietly, "you remember Madame Duval, don't you?"

Evangeline extended a limp hand. "Of course she does, *ma chère*," she said. "Once family, always family. Isn't that right, Lucille?"

Every muscle in my body tensed. Nobody called me Lucille. Nobody living, anyway. I forced a polite smile. "Please call me Boo. Everyone does. We're so glad you're here."

She looked past me as others emerged onto the porch. I couldn't tell if the turnout pleased or annoyed her.

As I struggled for what to say next, Delphine appeared with the tray bearing our mother's beautiful tea service.

"Welcome to Laguna Bay," she said in her sweetest voice. "Lila has told us how much you adore your tea. I'm quite a tea lover myself, so I took the liberty of preparing a pot of your favorite. Darjeeling, I believe? Do you take milk—"

"No, thank you," Evangeline said, cutting her off. "I would prefer something cold. Water will do."

My sister recovered quickly. She whisked the tray back into the house so fast I was probably the only one who noticed the tremble in her smile.

The old woman leaned in and whispered to my daughter.

"Is there somewhere Grandmama may sit?" Lila asked.

A few choice locations came to mind, but I kept them to myself. I swallowed my frustration over the insult to my sister and forged ahead. "While Delphine is getting your water, perhaps Merle can put your luggage inside. Lila and I will take you around back, where we've assembled a welcome reception in your honor."

Drawing on every diplomatic bone in my body, I did my best to treat Evangeline like the VIP she clearly believed herself to be. I sat her at the table with our council elders, where she immediately insisted on relocating Lila from my table to hers.

Poor Lila seemed willing to do whatever the old woman asked.

Delphine appeared with a tall glass of water the moment Evangeline sat down and set it in front of her. Instead of thanking her, Evangeline leaned toward Lila and whispered something behind her hand.

My daughter flushed through three distinct shades of mortification before saying, "Grandmama was wondering if some other refreshment might be available."

Oh, for crying out loud.

As Delphine sputtered, I plastered on my brightest fake smile and steered my sister toward a chair. Then I assured Evangeline I'd find something.

I considered it a personal triumph that I made it all the way into the kitchen and buried my head in the refrigerator before that smile gave way to a few choice mutterings.

"Need some help?"

I spun around to find Jemma lingering between the kitchen and living room, her expression hovering between sympathy and amusement.

"Sorry," I said, heat creeping up the back of my neck. "I thought everyone was outside."

"It's just me," Jemma said, pressing a hand to her stomach. "I'm not feeling great. Are you looking for something?"

"Her Majesty wants something cold that isn't water. I hope she likes lemonade." I grabbed the pitcher from the fridge. As I pulled a glass from the cupboard, I glanced back at Jemma and frowned. "You didn't have any of Delphine's vegan cheesecake, did you?"

Jemma chuckled lightly. "No. I woke up with it, but you guys were counting on these flowers and I didn't want to let you down." She looked out the window at the festivities. "I may bug out early."

"Sorry you'll miss the party." I was a little jealous. She wouldn't have to deal with that royal pain holding court in the backyard.

As I poured Evangeline's lemonade, Jemma tightened her hold on her stomach.

"Are you okay?" I asked. "Can I get you something?"

She winced. "Do you have anything for an upset stomach?"

"I'm sure we do." I put the pitcher away, then went to see what I could find in the medicine cabinet.

When I returned a few minutes later with several options, Jemma was even paler than before. I offered to drive her home, but she assured me she could handle it. So, I sent her on her way with everything I thought might be useful, then headed back outside with Evangeline's lemonade.

Surprisingly, the woman's spirits had noticeably improved. Maybe it was because a plate had appeared in front of her and she was nibbling the corner of a chicken taco.

Someone—Merle, probably—queued up soft jazz on the stereo, and the music drifted through the yard as people relaxed into their chairs. Conversation loosened. Laughter bubbled up around the tables.

As darkness fell, the temperature dipped, but light jackets and the outdoor heaters were more than sufficient to keep us warm, and no one rushed to go inside as the hours slipped by.

And yet.

Despite the easy chatter and the comfortable glow, I couldn't shake the feeling that something wasn't quite right.

Cornelia barely spoke at all. Instead, she let Howard and Neal carry the conversation while she simply watched Evangeline in that inscrutable way of hers. And theirs was more forced and stilted than usual.

Claire's earlier sparkle dimmed as the evening deepened. Twice I caught her standing at the edge of the yard, staring at an empty patch of grass near the avocado tree, her gaze distant and unfocused. I told myself she was probably just feeling like the new kid in town.

Both times, someone eventually pulled her back into the group. Once it was Willa, who drifted over and gently steered her back toward the others. The other time it was Howard. From the sharp tilt of Claire's shoulders and the tight set of Howard's jaw, I suspected harsh words had passed between them. But they were too far away, and I'd been too busy playing hostess, to be certain.

Still, by the time the desserts were rolled out—mini apple pies, shortbread, lemon bars, and, yes, Delphine's vegan cheesecake—I could have sworn I saw the faintest smile tug at the corner of Evangeline's mouth. I was halfway through my second lemon bar when she lifted her chin toward my sister.

"I'll take that tea now," she said. "If it isn't too much trouble."

"Of course," Delphine replied, ever gracious, and excused herself to the kitchen to prepare it.

Moments later, Claire delivered the tray with the fresh pot, while Delphine, I noticed, remained inside.

If Evangeline noticed the hand-off, she didn't mention it. She thanked Claire and sipped delicately.

Something about the moment weighed on me—a faint sense of wrongness that set me on edge.

Then Evangeline leaned in and whispered in Lila's ear. Whatever she said hardened Lila's expression. When Evangeline pulled back, Lila caught her arm and murmured a reply. For a split second, I thought I saw the old woman's composure crack, but it was gone just as quickly.

Evangeline gave Lila a smile, or maybe a smirk. Then she set her teacup down and rose to her feet. The chatter around the tables faded.

"I would like to propose a toast," she said, lifting her teacup once more. Her cool, appraising gaze swept over the gathering. "To my hosts—and to the community of Laguna Bay—"

Her voice faltered.

The teacup trembled in her hand.

Then it slipped from her fingers and shattered against the table in a spray of porcelain.

"Grandmama?" Lila's chair pushed back.

The old woman swayed once... twice... then collapsed.

For one frozen heartbeat, no one moved.

Then chaos erupted. Chairs scraped. Voices screeched. Glass splintered.

"Call the paramedics!" I yelled as I lunged forward, my pulse hammering.

That's when I noticed Kheppy race through her cat door from the house and bound across the yard. In a moment she was by Evangeline's side, then mine. Her voice cut through the noise. "Boo," she whispered to me, her laser gaze fixed on the old woman. "It's too late. She's gone."

Chapter 3

Rattled Nerves

GENTLE KNUCKLES TAPPED AGAINST my bedroom door. "Boo?" Merle's voice came through, low but steady. "You decent?"

The clock on the nightstand read a quarter till nine, but my body would've sworn it was much later.

Kheppy lifted her head from the pillow beside me, her amber eyes soft but alert. "I can tell him you need more time."

Part of me wanted to take her up on the offer—to tell her to send him away and let me disappear a while longer. After the police were called and nothing could be done for Evangeline, I'd come in here to collect my thoughts and somehow ended up collapsing on the bed instead.

Kheppy had quietly slipped in behind me and curled up against my side. Her warmth and low, rumbling purr soothed me.

"Boo?" Merle's voice came again. "May I come in?"

I couldn't hide forever. And if someone had to pull me out of my misery, I was glad it was him.

"Go ahead," I said, sitting up and trying to compose myself.

Merle eased the door open and peeked inside. "Detective Ernie Platt is here. I thought you'd want to know before he comes looking for you."

That snapped me out of my pity party. "Platt? He's back?"

Merle gave me a funny look. "It was only a vacation."

That's what the man had called it, but it had come on the heels of the last murder investigation. The timing made me wonder if he was quietly job-hunting.

"Anyway, he's here," Merle said. "You ready to talk?"

Hardly, but when did that ever stop me? I swung my legs off the bed and sat for a moment, waiting for the motivation to catch up.

Kheppy nudged my hand, and I obliged, letting my fingers sink into her fur.

"You should go," she urged. "The detective might think you have something to hide."

I pulled my hand back. "That's not funny."

"I wasn't joking," she said.

When Merle sat on the bed, his nearness almost undid me.

"You hanging in there?" he asked, his gaze finding mine.

I ran a hand through what was surely an epic case of bedhead. "Barely. Why's the detective here, anyway? She was eighty-five. It must have been a heart attack from the strain of the flight or something, right?"

Merle shrugged. "The police chief probably wants everything done by the book, considering she's from a prominent family."

Running the police department's Retired and Senior Volunteer Program meant Merle had a pretty good sense of how the place worked.

"You mean he doesn't want to get sued," I said.

"Yeah, basically," he agreed.

At least he was honest.

"Who has the detective talked to so far?"

A faint smirk tugged at his cheek. "He got an earful from Cornelia."

I gave up on my hair and straightened my collar. "I can imagine how well that went."

As the town's ever-meddling newspaper publisher, Cornelia never missed a chance to wedge herself into anything that smelled like scandal.

"Let's just say it was a short conversation," Merle said. "Delphine tried to walk the detective through what happened, but he seemed more interested in questioning the people seated at Evangeline's table."

"Lila?" I asked. I should have seen that coming, but the thought of my daughter being questioned by the police, even that lanky Columbo knockoff, made my stomach twist. "Is she still upset?"

Merle's head did a half-wobble that said the answer was a definite maybe.

That was enough to get me moving. "All right," I said as I pushed to my feet. "Let's get this over with."

When we stepped into the hallway, Lila was waiting just outside the door like she'd been listening. She somehow looked smaller than before, swallowed up in one of my old cardigans, her eyes red-rimmed and her bangs frizzed by the damp coastal night air.

"Hey," I said softly.

"Hey," she echoed, the word hardly making it past her lips.

For a moment, I thought—hoped—she might lean in for a hug. Instead, her gaze slid past me to the glow of the kitchen, and she kept her distance.

"How could this happen?" she whispered, brushing at her cheek with the back of her hand.

"I don't know, honey," I said. "But whatever you need, I'm here. We all are."

She drew in a careful breath and nodded.

I managed what I hoped passed for a comforting smile. "Where's the detective?"

"Outside." After a beat, she added, "With Willa. By the tables."

I reached out to touch her shoulder, but she shifted away.

My heart broke a little, but I tried to cover it with a smile.

"You stay inside," I said. "I'll take care of it."

Outside, the temperature had dropped considerably. I pulled my denim jacket tighter, but it was little protection against the chill or the backyard's utter disarray.

Just hours ago, the place had glowed with party lights and cheerful decorations. Now, yellow police tape slashed across the tables, and overturned chairs stood as bitter reminders of how quickly the night had turned deadly.

Detective Ernie Platt stood on the porch by the buffet table in his trench coat, a notebook in one hand and a pen in the other. He glanced my way as I approached.

“My condolences, Ms. Boudreaux,” he said.

“We’ve been over this,” I said. “It’s Boo.”

He nodded, taking the correction, and continued, “I know this must be a difficult time.”

“Understatement,” I said, then blew a stray strand out of my eyes with a huff. “What do you need to know, Detective?”

He began his questions—methodical and practiced, yet polite. Had Evangeline shown any sign of illness? Where had I been when she collapsed?

“I was at another table, so I didn’t see everything,” I said. “One minute she was giving her speech, the next she was on the ground. It all happened fast. But why does that matter if she had a heart attack?”

He glanced up through his dark, bushy eyebrows. “It wasn’t a heart attack.”

“Okay. Stroke then,” I said.

The way he shook his head made me wish I’d stayed in my bedroom. “What do you think it was?”

“The medics reported some irregularities with the victim. Until the coroner says otherwise, we’re treating her death as suspicious,” he said. “I understand she was drinking from a fresh pot of tea when she collapsed. Who prepared it?"

"I did."

I whipped around to see Delphine approaching, calm as lemon balm. "It was plain Darjeeling," she said. "Your police people took the pot and the tea."

Detective Platt's pen scratched across the page again. "I'll make a note of it." He glanced at the garden. "What do you grow back there?"

"Vegetables and herbs mostly," Delphine said.

"Mostly?" Platt echoed.

"If you'd like a closer look, I can grab a flashlight and show you around," Delphine offered.

I didn't expect the detective to take her up on the offer, but he did, following my sister to the fenced garden like a bloodhound trailing a scent. I used the moment to slip away with the excuse of needing to tidy up.

As Delphine introduced Detective Platt to the lavender patch, I spotted Claire lingering in the moonlight near the hibiscus hedge. Her gaze darted between Evangeline's empty chair and her leather loafers. She appeared to be talking to herself, which set off my internal alarm bells.

I'd seen Merle carry on plenty of one-sided conversations with Rupert, his ghostly best friend. Claire talking to spirits didn't surprise me, but doing it with police nearby was reckless.

I was about to remind her of that when she strode off toward the trail that wound up into the foothills. Fine, as long as the police couldn't see her—and none of them had seemed to—she could chat with the spirit world all she liked.

I headed back to the house to check on Lila.

When Delphine's garden tour wrapped up, I figured the detective would want to ask me more questions, but instead he checked in with Howard then Neal, who kept tugging at his turtleneck like it was irritating his gills.

When Detective Platt finally returned to me, his tone had changed.

"I didn't realize the victim was your mother-in-law," he said. "Was your relationship cordial?"

I hesitated. "Cordial, yes." Barely. "It's complicated."

The detective nodded as if he understood. But how could someone who didn't even have crow's-feet yet possibly understand?

"Would you describe her arrival here as difficult?" he pressed.

"That's one word for it," I said.

His pen scratched another note, the sound sharp against the quiet. I felt a flash of *déjà vu*. I'd been a murder suspect before, and I wasn't eager to relive the experience.

Still, the sooner he asked his questions, the sooner he'd get past the notion.

Eventually, Detective Platt finished his interviews and sent most of the party guests home. Everyone looked drained. Even the moon seemed to sag under the weight of it all.

Uniformed officers were still combing the patio when one of them called out, "Detective, we just got a call from the morgue, and the early test results are in."

"And?" the detective asked.

"Looks like poison," the guy said, "but more tests are needed to confirm it."

Poison? My heart jumped a beat.

The news didn't sit well with Platt, either. He rubbed his day-old stubble. "Any idea what kind?"

"Not yet," the tech added. "Just that it was ingested."

Platt glanced at me.

"She only picked at her plate," I said defensively.

He looked back at the tech. "Put together a list of everything the victim ate and drank tonight."

Once we finished the list, I expected more questions, but was relieved when he looked up with a weak smile. "Thank you. You've been very helpful. Would you mind if I looked around a bit more?"

"Go right ahead," I said. "I'm going to fix myself some tea. Can I get you something?"

He shook his head, so I left him to it.

In the kitchen, I stood at the sink near the open window with my tea, looking out at a fog bank clinging to the hillside. The yard felt hollow and strange. Only a couple of uniformed officers remained, and they had retreated to the cars parked in the driveway. The crime-scene techs huddled near their van.

All the laughter, the lights, the warmth that had filled the backyard earlier in the evening seemed like a fleeting dream.

I could see Lila and Delphine sitting on the steps, illuminated by the moonlight, their voices drifting on the breeze.

"But I shouldn't have said it," Lila was saying, her tone low and raw.

My ears perked. She didn't know I was near.

"I'd do anything to take it back," she continued. "I wish I'd never said it."

Delphine touched her back. "It was the stress, dear. You didn't mean it."

"I never should have threatened her, Aunt Del," Lila whispered. "I was just so mad."

The words hit me like a gunshot. But not just me.

"Miss Sage?" Detective Platt emerged sharply from the other end of the porch. He must have been hidden in the shadows and blocked from my view by the window frame.

The look on my daughter's face said plainly his presence was a surprise to her too.

"You didn't mention that you and the victim had argued before she collapsed. Why not?" He moved closer to Lila.

My daughter rose and stared at him, her eyes wide. "That's not what I meant," she said. "We were... She was..." She clamped her mouth shut and shook her head.

I rushed out the back door to protect her. "It's all right, honey. Whatever happened, just tell him."

But my daughter said nothing.

The detective sighed, the sound heavy with fatigue. He seemed as worn down as the rest of us.

"Lila, please," I begged her. "Talk to him."

She ignored me and stared straight ahead with a cold, dead gaze.

"I'm sorry, Boo," the detective said, "but if she won't cooperate, I have to take her in. Maybe she'll be more cooperative at the station."

"Detective, no," I pleaded. "She's distraught. She just lost her grandmother."

For a moment, there was something almost like regret in his eyes.

"I have to," he said. "This isn't an arrest—not yet—but I can't ignore what I heard."

He turned back to Lila, giving her one last chance.

"Lila, please," I begged. "Just answer his questions."

She looked at me, then at the detective. Then, slowly—so slowly—she shook her head.

Before I could plead again, he signaled to the officers nearby. They stepped forward, and one of them took Lila by the arm.

Her eyes were wide, fear written across her face as she turned to me.

"Mom," she whispered. "I would never hurt her. You have to believe me."

My throat locked. "I do. It'll be okay. We'll figure this out."

They led her to a patrol car. The slam of the door echoed down the quiet street. For a moment, everything inside me went still. Then the ordinary noises of the world came rushing back—the crickets, the rustle of the avocado tree's leaves, the crunch of tires rolling down our dirt lane.

When everyone else retreated to the house, Kheppy pressed against my ankle.

"They will see reason, Boo," my feline friend whispered.

I wanted to believe her. I tried.

Instead, I felt that electric hum of injustice as the realization settled on me that if what the detective had said was true, then someone had killed Evangeline Duval here on my property and right under my own nose.

And it wasn't my daughter. I knew that. I could feel it in my blood and my bones.

I picked up Kheppy. Her fur bristled slightly as she stared along the fence line.

"You feel it too?" I asked.

She nodded. "Something is wrong."

Wrong didn't even begin to describe it.

Kheppy's tail swayed. "What will you do?"

I drew a shaky breath as my fear for my daughter hardened into resolve.

"I have a terrible feeling that as long as they have Lila, they're going to focus on her instead of finding the killer," I said. "Which means if they don't, it's going to be up to me."

I swallowed. "I have to protect my daughter."

Chapter 4

Mysterious Plus-One

As Detective Platt drove away with Lila, he may as well have taken me with him. I stood on the porch like a sleepwalker, watching the taillights disappear into the darkness. My body was still upright, but everything inside me lagged several beats behind.

Merle tried to reassure me. He said once Lila got to the station, she'd realize the detective wasn't fooling around, and she'd give her statement. Everything would be all right. I knew he meant well—my head understood that—but my heart was still sinking.

Delphine must have sensed it.

She slipped an arm through Merle's and drew him back inside with a question about a "tricky" pilot light on the stove—though she knew perfectly well how to make it catch.

Whatever she said to him in a low voice worked because a few minutes later he came back out, wrapped me in a hug, and promised he'd head to the station to keep an eye on Lila.

"Thank you," I said, grateful for his ability to be a Stetson-wearing fly on that particular wall.

"It's been a long day," he said, brushing my hair back from my face. "Promise you'll get some rest."

"I promise," I said. Whether it was true or not felt beside the point.

His goodbye kiss was quick but sweet, and he gave my hand one last squeeze before heading for his truck, leaving me alone on the porch.

When I finally wandered back inside, Delphine had already shed her party clothes in favor of pajamas and a comfy robe. She offered to brew a fresh pot of chamomile. I told her no.

She ignored me, of course, drifting back into the kitchen as if she hadn't heard me.

While she worked on the tea, I retrieved my *Hocus Focus* notebook and flipped it open. It had brought me a strange sort of luck the last time I found myself tangled in a homicide investigation, and at this point, I wasn't above superstition. I put pen to paper and jotted down the names of the party guests—any one of them could be a suspect—then hesitated.

The ink blotted where my hand paused, my handwriting already starting to wobble—fatigue, nerves, the weight of the night. Take your pick.

"Do you think the tarot cards might help?" Delphine asked as she set the pot beside me and grabbed two fresh mugs.

I glared up from my notes. "I'll stick with the notebook," I said. I didn't want to take any chances when Lila's freedom might be on the line.

I dragged a line alongside the list of names. "One of these people might have killed Evangeline," I said, hearing the tired rasp in my voice.

As I stared at the list, one name—one face, in fact—kept pushing its way to the forefront of my thoughts. Claire Greenwood.

Del poured the tea into the cups.

"You promised Merle you would rest," she said as she handed me one. "We can sort this out in the morning."

"Morning is just a few hours away." I sipped, welcoming its warm comfort. "I'm not wasting that time on sleep."

She sighed—the long-suffering kind that said *Here we go again*. "Fine. But use the cards. Maybe they'll—"

"No." The word came out sharper than I'd intended. I softened it with a breath. "Not tonight." If she thought I'd changed my mind about trusting the cards, now she knew better. I hadn't, and I wouldn't.

Delphine's brows knit. "Didn't they help last time?"

"They did." Sort of. I stared at the notebook, the neat list of names beginning to blur. "But they were vague, or they didn't tell me the whole truth." Or maybe I'd been too quick to jump to conclusions. All were possibilities.

Even if they had helped, their betrayal still stung. Once I'd trusted them to show me the truth. Instead, they'd shown me only one truth among many possibilities—and I'd paid for that mistake for years.

So, no, I wasn't ready to go back down that road. Ordinary logic would work fine.

I tapped the pen against the first name. "All right. Let's think it through. Neal Glory. He was sitting beside her. He could easily have slipped her the poison."

Delphine frowned. "Why would he, though?"

"He knew she was trying to turn the High Council against us," I said. "If she'd succeeded, we could lose our charter and our protection as a sanctuary."

"We all know that," she said. "At least everyone at the Midnight Council meeting. We all have just as much to lose."

It was true.

"Howard and Cornelia were at the table too," she added.

I tapped my pen beside his name. "I saw Howard snap at Claire. Did you see that?"

"No. He seemed a little out of sorts, but come on—it's Howard. I really can't see him killing anyone. What about Cornelia?"

She had a point. Cornelia definitely seemed the most likely suspect, but I had my reservations.

"Poisoning doesn't seem her style." Still, I made a note beside her name. Something about the way she'd stared silent daggers at Evangeline all night didn't sit right with me.

As we worked through the list of suspects from Evangeline's table, we both knew Lila wasn't among them. And

I was certain my sister would agree, that was how it should be.

"You and I sat at the next table," she continued, "with Merle, Opal, and Willa."

After Jemma left, Delphine had moved him to the open seat. Whether she was trying to bring him closer to me or farther from Claire, I wasn't entirely sure, but I appreciated the effort.

I stared at the names.

"Why are you shaking your head?" my sister asked.

"Poisoning feels personal, doesn't it?" I asked. "But except for me and the elders, no one in Laguna Bay had ever met Evangeline before tonight. Not even you."

Delphine took another sip. The cup clinked softly as she set it back on its saucer. "That's true. But why do you think that matters?"

I tapped my pen again. "I don't know. It just doesn't feel right."

"What does your gut tell you?" she pressed.

I flipped to a fresh page and wrote a name across the top: Claire Greenwood.

My sister's eyebrows arched. "Are you sure you're not letting your jealousy get the better of you?"

"No," I said honestly. I hadn't seen any more flirting with Merle, but it was late, and I'd drunk enough chamomile tea to fill a bathtub. Even so, I couldn't shake the feeling that something about her odd, anti-social behavior tonight didn't add up.

"She seems harmless enough," my sister said. "And she wasn't sitting anywhere near Evangeline's table."

"Is she harmless? She delivered the tea to Evangeline." I chewed my lip. "And what do we really know about her? She's only been here a few years. And after it happened—while the forensic techs were bagging evidence and taking photos—I saw her out past the garden. She was acting strange. Like she was talking to ghosts."

"She's a medium, Boo," my sister added. "That's her thing."

"Maybe," I said. "But something about it felt wrong. Reckless even. And there was that argument with Howard."

A sharp knock rattled the front door. Both of us jumped. Even Kheppy lifted her sleepy head.

"Did the police say they were coming back?" Delphine pulled her robe tighter. "Maybe they've—"

"Don't say it," I warned. I couldn't bear more bad news. I crossed the room, heart hammering, and cracked the door.

Merle stood on the porch, cowboy hat in hand. Relief washed through me—then it curdled into worry.

"Is there news about Lila?"

He shook his head. "Nothing yet. I was there, but I couldn't find out anything."

The breath I'd been holding escaped in a rush. "Did you see her?"

"I tried to pretend I was looking for next week's volunteer schedule," he said with a faint shake of his head. "Not sure I fooled anyone, but they let me through. She looks all right."

I stepped aside to let him in. "Thank you. But you could've called."

"I know." His gaze drifted to the cluttered table. "I was going to. Then I saw your lights were still on."

We both knew my place wasn't on his way home from the station.

"You said you were going to get some rest," he added gently, looking down at me—only mildly reproachful. "So, what are you doing?"

"Trying to sort out what happened," I said. "We were just talking about Claire."

"The pet cemetery gal?" He rubbed his jaw. "What about her?"

"She gave the tea to Evangeline," I said.

He nodded.

"I also saw her standing off by herself while everyone was eating, and she was acting like she was talking to a ghost. Did you see anything?"

He frowned and scratched the side of his neck. "No, but she sees animal spirits. That's not really what I do."

Was there a difference? "What about Rupert? Did he see anything?" I asked.

He shrugged. "I doubt it. He hasn't been around all day."

Kheppy perked up. "I saw that woman walking with a cat. A white Persian cat."

I stared at my furry friend. "You saw Claire with a cat? When?"

"After Evangeline collapsed," Kheppy said. "They were standing beyond the garden. I noticed you looking in that direction. I was going to welcome her, but Delphine called me into the kitchen for a nibble of chicken."

I remembered the moment. "I saw Claire, but I didn't see a cat." A chill crept up my spine. "Was it a spirit?"

Kheppy had seen human ghosts before, so the idea of her seeing an animal spirit wasn't far-fetched. Still, she hesitated.

"She appeared solid to me," Kheppy said. "But perhaps not." Her whiskers twitched. "I would need to see her again to be certain. And I would like to know if she is the source."

"The source of what?" I asked.

Kheppy leaped onto the windowsill above the kitchen sink and stared at the moonlit yard. "I felt something in the air. At the time, I didn't understand it. But now..." She turned back to us, her eyes glowing like burnished gold. "It was a kind of pain I've never experienced before—and it may have come from that cat."

"Pain?" Delphine echoed. "Do you mean physical or emotional pain?"

"I cannot say," Kheppy said softly. "It may be one. Or the other. Or both."

Merle rubbed the back of his neck. "So you think this cat was a spirit?"

"I didn't know it then," Kheppy admitted. "But if none of you saw her, she must have been." Her tail swished.

A ghost cat. Just what my night needed.

I sank onto the sofa, my notebook still clenched in my hand. "Well, Kheppy, I suppose we can add medium to your already impressive list of talents."

Kheppy hopped onto my lap and sniffed delicately. "I suppose you can."

An unsettling thought lodged itself in my mind.

"If Claire brought a spirit with her," I said slowly, "why wouldn't she mention it? Does that strike anyone else as strange?"

The room went quiet except for the hum of the refrigerator and the rhythmic tick of the mantel clock.

Merle settled on the arm of a chair. "What are you thinking?"

"That I need to talk to Claire," I said. "I want to find out more about her and her mysterious plus-one."

He glanced at the dark window. "Not tonight. You'll only spook her if you go now."

"I know." I rubbed my temples, the adrenaline finally ebbing, leaving exhaustion in its wake.

"A few hours won't change anything," he murmured.

Maybe not. But waiting felt like surrender. Every instinct I had urged me to do something, to grab hold of the truth before it slipped away.

Still, I nodded.

Merle walked over and gave my shoulder a gentle squeeze. “Try to rest, Boo. Really.”

After he left, the silence crept back in—thick, heavy, and full of unanswered questions.

Delphine headed down the hall. “I’m going to lie down. You should too.”

“I will,” I lied.

Once she was gone, Kheppy crawled onto my chest so we were nose to nose. “You won’t rest until you find whoever did this, will you?” she asked quietly.

I stroked the soft spot between her ears. My wise little friend knew me far too well.

Chapter 5

Resting Place

THE SIGN ON THE locked door of the Hearts and Halos Pet Cemetery office read: Business Hours 8 a.m. to 5 p.m.

I jabbed a finger at it. "See? It should be open."

Kheppy shifted in my arms and let out a wide yawn, her tiny pink tongue curling.

"But she is not here. You could have let me sleep."

"That would make one of us," I muttered.

I hadn't slept at all. I'd spent the night waiting by the phone for a call telling me I could pick up Lila from the station. But it never came.

I'd convinced myself that Lila would come to her senses. She had to see she was only hurting herself by staying silent. I figured she would realize that once she spent enough time in that cold, stark place.

The hours had slipped by with no word from the detective. I'd even tried calling him for an update, but so far those calls had been ignored.

Which left me with too much time to obsess over the case and Claire Greenwood—the pet cemetery owner Kheppy had seen with a ghost cat just before she served

Evangeline the tea, which may have contained the poison that killed her.

Claire had never struck me as the vengeful type. But I'd been wrong before.

I didn't know what she could have had against Evangeline—beyond the general threat she posed to Laguna Bay—but Claire's odd behavior, her tiff with Howard, and her proximity to the tea, pushed her straight to the top of my suspect list.

And right now, she felt like my best lead.

I set Kheppy down on the porch railing and rubbed the stiffness in my shoulders. "We'll wait a few more minutes. Maybe she's running late." It had been a late night, after all. I pulled my phone from my purse. "I'll see if Merle has any news about Lila."

The screen glowed against my fingers as I paced and gazed at the morning fog still blurring the hillside beyond the fence.

Merle picked up on the second ring. "Morning, sunshine."

Despite my worries, I managed to smile. "They still haven't released Lila. Do you think that's a bad sign?"

I heard him sigh. "Let's not speculate," he said in that low and reassuring tone he used when he was trying to keep me calm. "I'm heading to the station now. I'll see what I can find out. Where are you?"

"Claire's. I wanted to talk to her about the cat Kheppy saw, but she's not here yet. If you see Lila, ask her if there's anything I can do. What about breakfast? Should I bring her something to eat?"

"Boo, they won't let you bring in food." There was that reassuring tone again.

"I'm not talking about a cake with a metal file baked inside. Maybe a fruit tart from the Scandinavian bakery. She loves those."

He chuckled. "No food. How's Claire's place look? I haven't been out there since she finished the renovation."

The building was the kind of restored, old-money beauty Laguna Bay loved to brag about—white trim, steep gables, and the faint chill of a place that had lived a dozen lives before becoming a pet cemetery. I let out a slow breath. "It's lovely. She did a nice job."

A small nose brushed my ankle. "Hold on, Merle." I pulled the phone from my ear and raised my eyebrows at my furry companion in a silent *What?*

Kheppy sat down and looked up, pleased with herself. "She's out there."

Following her gaze, I spotted a lone figure crossing the grassy field beyond the gate. It was Claire in a khaki coat, with a perky ponytail and a brisk, if uneasy stride.

"Gotta go, Merle. Call me if you get any news."

"You too." He hesitated. "Hey."

My heart skipped. Ever since our romance had rekindled, our goodbyes had become awkward little dances. Neither of us, it seemed, knew exactly how to take that next step. Would today be the day?

"Yeah?" I asked.

"Be careful," he said.

Nope. Not today.

"You too," I said and hung up before I could ruin it by saying something sappy.

I tucked my phone away and lifted a hand in greeting. Claire startled, glanced over her shoulder as if shooing someone I couldn't see, then pasted on a bright—too bright—smile and hurried toward the gate.

Before she reached us, Kheppy brushed against my leg again.

"I'll be back," she said, her tail swishing.

"Don't go too far," I murmured, but she was already padding across the grass toward the hedge. I'd learned long ago that when Kheppy wandered off, it usually meant she was answering nature's call.

When Claire drew closer, I met her halfway. "I hope I'm not catching you at a bad time," I said.

She shook her head. "Not at all. I like to walk the grounds before opening to check for any damage, and it's good exercise. I'm just running a little behind schedule today. Is something wrong?"

"I just wanted to check on you," I said. "Yesterday was difficult for all of us. I know you're still fairly new around here, and I'm so sorry you had to go through that."

The apology was genuine, but I was also hoping it might open the door to a conversation about her strange behavior at the party and her mysterious companion.

Her expression softened. "Oh, Boo, it wasn't your fault."

"Still, it mattered that you were there." I looked over my shoulder, back at the building. "And I had no idea you had done so much work on this place. It's gorgeous. The repairs, the paint, all of it."

The office and attached chapel gleamed in fresh white trimmed in moss green. Even the iron fence had been scrubbed to a dignified sheen. Beyond it, a sprawling green lawn was dotted with grave markers—tiny marble paws, brass plaques, concrete angels with tails. The sight pinched my heart.

"Thank you," Claire said, following my gaze. "It took longer than I expected, but I think it was worth it. I wanted it to be a truly lovely resting place for our creature companions."

"Our?" I asked lightly. "You have partners?"

Her cheeks colored. "No, I just mean me... and some friends who helped out."

"The spirits?" I said in a low voice.

Her relief was palpable. "Of course you understand. Most people don't."

"Always safer to be cautious," I said.

Her smile faded, and her gaze lowered. "I heard the police took Lila in," she said. "You must be so worried."

The pain locked in my chest nearly broke free. I shoved it back. This wasn't the moment to fall apart.

"Routine questioning," I said. "Lila would never hurt her grandmother. She wouldn't hurt anyone."

"Of course she wouldn't." Claire's eyes were open and earnest. "Everyone speaks so highly of her. I'm sure she'll be home soon."

"She will," I said, nodding as if sheer willpower could make it true.

I tried not to think of Lila sitting in a cold interrogation room or worse.

Claire stiffened and clasped her hands, as if she wasn't quite sure what to do with them. "I'd invite you in, but you probably have to get going. Businesses don't run themselves, do they?" She glanced at her watch, as if she were hoping I'd agree.

I felt the pull of Lila waiting at the police station—and the tug of the Boo-tique—but Merle was already on his way to the station and lately the shop seemed to run just fine whether I was there or not, which was a realization that stung more than I cared to admit.

Yet Claire's eagerness made me even more determined to figure out why she'd been so cagey the night before.

"I'm fine on time," I said.

Her polite smile faltered. "Was there something else you needed?"

"Actually, yes." I hesitated, then plunged ahead. "Kheppy thought she saw a cat with you last night."

Her brows lifted, then drew down into a scowl. "No. I didn't see any cats—just Kheppy. Sorry. She must have been mistaken."

Under normal circumstances, I would have accepted that. But after Evangeline's death, nothing felt normal.

"Are you sure? Could one of your... uh... residents have followed you?" I nodded toward the tidy rows of grave markers.

Claire shook her head. "No hitchhiking animal ghosts followed me to your house, if that's what you're asking."

That was exactly what I was asking. "I know it sounds silly. Sorry."

"It's all right." A brittle smile returned. "But I really should get inside. Can I walk you to your car?"

Defeated, I glanced around. "I just need to find Kheppy. She wandered off."

Then movement caught my eye, and from around the back of the building, Kheppy strutted toward us, tail held high, eyes glinting like fire. She looked thoroughly—and irritatingly—pleased with herself.

"Where have you been?" I asked as she approached.

"Meeting a new friend," she said.

"Really?" I looked around. I didn't see anyone. Kheppy was prone to mixing up her phrases, so I assumed this must be one of those moments.

The color drained from Claire's cheeks. Her hands clasped together until her knuckles went white.

Kheppy stopped a few feet away.

Her gaze fixed on the empty space beside her.

The air shimmered, like heat rising off asphalt.

Then the shimmer became a shape. Light folding into fur and form. A cat with long, fluffy white fur and a flat nose materialized, ghost-pale, her edges faintly luminous. Her iridescent eyes sparkled, full of intelligence.

I stared, my breath caught somewhere in my throat.

Kheppy inclined her head, regal as ever. "Allow me to introduce the former companion—and captive—of Evangeline Duval."

The ghost cat turned her gaze on me. When she spoke, her voice was soft, echoing faintly, as if carried through water.

"You may call me Saphira."

Chapter 6

Saphira

SITTING ON THE GRASSY lawn before me, Saphira's feline outline wavered unsteadily until her form slowly solidified. She settled primly beside Kheppy, her ghostly fur stirring in a breeze I couldn't feel. The sight rooted me in place.

She looked like something from a dream. Her fluffy tail curled neatly around her paws as she regarded me with a calm, thoughtful gaze—serene, knowing, and utterly mesmerizing.

Claire hovered beside me, hands fidgeting with her coat's collar.

"Why didn't you tell me?" I asked her, trying to understand how she could keep this secret.

"It wasn't my story to tell," she murmured, shifting her weight like each word was a pebble in her shoe.

Saphira turned her startling blue eyes toward Claire. The shimmer around her softened.

"Claire helped me," the ghost cat said, her voice layered with a soft, otherworldly resonance. "I was so lost, so confused when she found me."

I frowned. "Confused? How?"

The feline apparition lowered her chin. "When my mistress's life ended, the spell binding me to her broke. Without that tether, I drifted. Claire found me."

My breath caught as the revelation sank in. "Evangeline bound you?" I shook my head, disgust coursing through me.

The woman was a monster, but to imprison a sweet cat's spirit—why?

Kheppy's tail swished, her fur bristling with indignation. "Disgraceful woman," she muttered.

"I was her companion in life," Saphira said. "I passed not long after her son. She was already broken by that loss, and my death was more than she could bear."

That was hardly an excuse for such cruelty, but my thoughts had hooked on something else Saphira mentioned. The death of Evangeline's son.

Luc Duval.

A lifetime had passed since I had called him my husband, yet Saphira's reference to him still tightened something deep inside me. Luc and I had been divorced for nearly a decade when he died, but that hadn't lessened my grief.

And Evangeline... I'd always assumed her smothering devotion to him came from her need to control everything around her. It was part of the reason our marriage failed. After Luc died, she tightened that same grip on Lila.

I'd let Lila stay with the Duvals because it seemed like the right thing to do. The family had money, connections, a sprawling New Orleans estate filled with things I could never give my daughter—facts Evangeline reminded me of again and again. I told myself I was being unselfish.

But it tore me apart. Every single day.

So hearing that she'd used magic to bind this creature to her even after death horrified me, yes. But it didn't surprise me.

Claire cleared her throat and shifted awkwardly. "Perhaps we should take this conversation inside. I'd like to sit down, and I could use some coffee."

"I'll take tea if you've got it," I said.

We walked toward the back of the building. Cool moisture clung to the air, carrying the scent of damp grass and a faint hint of salt from the distant shoreline, even though we were tucked against the foothills, blocks from the beach.

Saphira glided more than she walked, each step leaving no mark upon the ground.

When Claire led us through the back door, I was surprised to enter not an office but a kitchen. Her renovation had clearly included a cozy living space.

She set a kettle on the stove and invited me to sit at the counter. As she pulled mugs from the cupboards, I tried—and failed—to stop staring at Saphira.

The cat's spirit hovered nearby, her outline faintly glowing at the edges. Each tiny shift of her fur sent rippling tendrils through the air that were mesmerizing to watch.

I liked to think nothing surprised me anymore. But a ghost cat? That was a new one.

"Black, green, or herbal?" Claire asked, offering a small basket filled with individually wrapped tea bags.

I thumbed through the selection and chose one labeled English Thunderbolt, figuring it had to be strong—and right now, the stronger the better.

Claire and I settled onto stools at the breakfast bar overlooking the sweeping lawn. Saphira floated to the counter's edge—graceful and spectral all at once—while Kheppy sat beside her, studying her.

Questions spun through me like leaves in a restless wind, none of them staying still long enough for me to decide which to ask first.

Claire broke the silence. "You're probably wondering how Saphira ended up here."

I let out a quiet huff of laughter. "That's definitely on the list."

My hostess no longer seemed pressed for time, which made me wonder if her earlier desire to get rid of me had nothing to do with work at all. Now that I knew about her ghostly friend, she seemed almost at ease as she wrapped both hands around her mug.

"Saphira approached me when I was at your place yesterday," she said. "I didn't say anything because..." She glanced down at the phantom feline. "Saphira, maybe you should explain."

Saphira edged closer to Kheppy.

"It's safe," my ancient companion said, lowering her head in a reassuring nod. "Boo is a friend."

My heart warmed, and I had to suppress the urge to pull Kheppy into my arms.

Claire's shoulders softened. "I know I can trust you. Willa always said you were someone I could turn to if anything ever went wrong, or if anything ever happened to her."

That caught me off guard. "I didn't realize you two were close."

"We are," Claire said as she crossed the room to pull back the curtains. Pale sunlight struggled to break through the gray clouds. "More like family, really. She and my grandmother were neighbors growing up."

Another surprise. "Oh? Was that around here?"

"Up near Lake Tahoe. That's where our families are from. Willa moved here after college. She always made Laguna Bay sound like paradise, so when I was ready for a change, I knew it was the place for me."

Funny. I'd known Willa my entire life. I'd always assumed she was as much a Laguna Bay native as I was.

Apparently not.

The kettle whistled sharply. Claire grabbed it and poured the steaming water into my cup. The tea leaves bloomed at once, releasing a fragrant steam that tickled my nose.

Saphira drifted to the window bench and began kneading the cushion, her translucent paws moving in a familiar rhythm. Though they left no impression on the fabric, the motion seemed to soothe her.

When she noticed me watching, heat rushed to my cheeks, and I looked away, as if I'd intruded on something private.

"It's all right," she mewed, her voice still weak but gaining strength. "You are curious?"

"Yes," I said. "I just can't imagine what you must have gone through. That must have been awful."

The ghost cat mulled the question, then said, "I do not remember all of it. When my mistress died and I was no longer bound to her, I found freedom disorienting. She had controlled me for so long, I felt completely dependent upon her magic."

"It was cruel," I said. "Why did she do it?"

Saphira's ears twitched. "I have often wondered. After Luc died, she fell into a deep sadness. When I died, those feelings twisted into something more desperate and fearful. It was not long after that she performed the binding ritual."

I'd always blamed Evangeline for her cruelty. I'd never considered the fear beneath it—the way love, twisted by grief, might turn possessive and desperate. Not that it excused anything she'd done. But the jagged pieces of her life were beginning to fit together, forming a picture darker—and far sadder—than I'd ever imagined.

Claire reached out as if to touch Saphira, then stopped herself. Her hand drifted through empty air. "I saw Saphira at the party, before... the accident," she said.

Accident? I suppose Evangeline's poisoning might have been a mistake, though it seemed pretty deliberate to me.

"I could tell something wasn't right," Claire continued. "But the binding spell prevented her from speaking of it. It wasn't until afterward—when Saphira explained her circumstances—that I understood."

Claire swallowed hard, fighting against emotion. "That's when I invited her here."

A soft chime pinged from Claire's phone before I could ask if Saphira intended to stay. Claire tapped the screen, and a security feed from the front of the building appeared.

An old Cadillac had pulled into the parking area. An elderly man climbed out from the driver's side and helped an elderly woman from the passenger's side.

"That would be the Bennetts," Claire said. "They have an appointment to discuss options for their departed cocker spaniel."

I tried to catch Kheppy's eye, but her attention remained fixed on Saphira.

"We need to go, Khep," I whispered.

Kheppy glanced at me as though she'd forgotten I was there. Then she gave herself a small shake, as if clearing her thoughts, and hopped down, landing lightly on the tile floor.

Saphira turned to Kheppy. "I hope we will speak again."

"We will," Kheppy assured her. "I'll make sure of it."

When I thanked Claire for the tea and her time, she hugged me unexpectedly and whispered, "Thank you."

"For what?" I asked.

"For your kindness."

I didn't know what to say to that, so I squeezed her hand and stepped outside into the still, gray morning.

As Kheppy and I walked to the car, a breeze swept through the parking lot, sending dried leaves skittering across the asphalt like the questions swirling in my mind.

About Claire.

About Saphira.

About Evangeline's death.

About Lila.

Especially Lila.

I slid behind the wheel as Kheppy hopped into the passenger seat.

"Did you sense the source of what you felt last night?" I asked quietly.

Kheppy considered it for a moment. "In a way, yes. One of them has been touched by it, though I do not yet understand how. That is all I know."

Her ears tilted back. "Is there any news about Lila?"

I wanted more answers, but if she had them, she would have said so.

I lifted my phone and scrolled through my messages. "Let's see," I said, checking for anything from Merle or a reply from Detective Platt. Nothing.

I tried Platt again, but the call went straight to voicemail. There was no point leaving another message when he hadn't returned the last one. I sent Merle a quick text, then counted to thirty before deciding I'd had enough of this waiting game.

I started the car and pulled onto the road.

The station was next.

Waiting was no longer an option.

Chapter 7
In Holding

THE CAR BESIDE ME in the Laguna Bay Police Station parking lot chirped an electronic *beep-beep* as I killed my engine, jolting my nerves enough to make me jump in my seat. Perfect. As if I needed a shot of adrenaline on top of the caffeine already coursing through my veins after that high-octane tea at Claire's.

My neighbor's headlights winked to life as a woman approached it with her key fob in hand. I gripped the steering wheel and waited until she pulled away.

The clock on the car's dashboard read a quarter to nine. The Boo-tique didn't open until ten, which should be enough time to find out why I couldn't get an update on Lila. Detective Platt had said he only needed her statement, but this delay had me concerned. Was he planning to use that stupid comment against my sweet girl, as I'd feared?

The gentle weight of Kheppy's white paw on my thigh pulled me out of my spiral.

"Breathe," she said, gazing up at me with kind, tawny eyes as a warm purr vibrated through her. "It will be all right."

I scooped her up and held her to my chest. "What would I do without you, my wise old friend?"

"Let's hope neither of us has to find out any time soon," she said. "Perhaps you should tell Sissy you may be late, though."

Like I said, wise.

"You're right. If I get tied up here, I don't want her to worry." I dug for my phone and dialed the shop to leave a message.

Sissy picked up on the second ring. "Boo? Everything okay?"

"What are you doing there?" I sputtered. "We don't open for another hour."

"I had the most adorable idea for a Thanksgiving window display," she said. "So I came in early to get started. I hope that's okay."

"Is that okay? It's fantastic." I'd been meaning to redo that window for days.

"Don't worry about a thing," she said. "The cash register is ready, and I've even got the shop's protection candle burning. Take your time. Family comes first."

My throat tightened. For a moment, I couldn't speak. Of all the things I'd expected today, being knocked sideways by gratitude hadn't been on the list.

"Thank you," I finally managed. "You're a treasure, you know that?"

"Aww." I could hear her smile. "You're making me blush. Get here when you can. Good luck."

When I hung up, I set the phone in my lap and leaned back with a slow exhale. "Sissy really is one in a million."

Kheppy nodded. "A rough diamond."

I rolled my lips inward to keep from grinning. "I think you mean a diamond in the rough."

She swished her tail. "That is what I said."

I was about to stand my ground, but I figured I'd let her have this one. There were times when it was important to be right, but this wasn't one of them. I opened the car door, and cold morning air brushed my cheeks. "Sit tight, okay?"

"Gladly," she purred and curled into a furry little ball on the passenger seat. "I shall guard the vehicle."

I smiled despite my nerves, shut the door, and headed toward the station's lobby entrance.

Inside, the lights blazed in a way that made the whole place feel sterile and overly alert. The bitter stench of burned coffee wafted from somewhere behind the counter.

As I stepped into the short line to speak to the clerk, my heart thudded. I kept telling myself to stay calm. There was no reason to think Lila was anything but fine. There was probably a reasonable explanation for why she was still here.

All that self-talk did nothing to make me feel better. Not really.

When the clerk behind the clear acrylic window finally called me forward, my pulse was racing so fast I was almost dizzy.

The young man glanced up from his computer keyboard, and recognition lit up his face. "Nice to see you again, Ms. Boudreaux."

Lovely. Just what every law-abiding resident wants to hear.

"I'm here to see my daughter, Lila Sage," I said. "She's with Detective Platt."

He checked his clipboard.

His eyebrows drew together.

And just like that, the friendly smile slid right off his face.

"Oh," he said.

That single syllable hollowed me out. "What does that mean—oh?"

He glanced over his shoulder. "She's in holding."

My stomach dropped.

"I need to see if she's allowed visitors."

That didn't sound like she was here giving a statement. Before I could ask the clerk why she would be in holding, he stood and disappeared into one of the offices along the wall.

I dug my fingernails into my palms to keep from trembling. All around me, the station bustled—radios crackling, doors slamming, phones ringing—while I stood there waiting to see my daughter.

When the clerk reappeared, his smile was tight and strained. "If you could take a seat, someone will be with you in a moment."

"Is she okay?" I demanded.

He hesitated, and that was worse than any answer. "Someone will be here in a moment," he repeated.

I took a seat because my legs were shaking so badly I wasn't sure I could trust them. The vinyl chair squeaked as I settled into it.

Something wasn't right. Deep in my gut, I felt it.

Finally, Detective Platt appeared, his white dress shirt already rumpled, a yellow notepad tucked under his arm.

"Ms. Boudreaux?"

I was on my feet instantly. "Is my daughter all right?"

"Of course," he said. "She's fine."

"I want to see her." I tried to keep my emotions in check.

"You will," he said. "I just have a few questions first."

He led me into a small room furnished with nothing but a table and two chairs facing each other. An interrogation room, plain as day.

"Have a seat," he said and took one of the chairs for himself. He set his notepad on the table, flipped it open, and began scribbling before I'd even settled into the chair on the opposite side of the table.

"Why did your daughter come to Laguna Bay?" he asked without preamble.

"To see me," I said, shifting on the unforgiving metal seat. "I'm sure I mentioned that last night."

"How long had it been since you'd seen her before yesterday?"

"Ten years," I said. "I also told you that. I'm sure Lila has as well."

He didn't respond. He just wrote.

Then he looked up. "No. Lila hasn't answered any of my questions. She's refused to speak at all."

My pulse stumbled. "Why?"

"You'd have to ask her."

"I will. Let me talk to her."

His jaw tightened, just slightly—but enough.

"I'll see what I can do," he said at last. He stood and left the room, the door shutting firmly behind him.

I stared at the faux-wood grain of the table, at the faint scratches etched into its surface. My breath dragged through my chest.

Why was Lila still refusing to talk? What could she possibly have to hide?

The door opened again, and Detective Platt reentered.

"You can speak to her," he said, "but please tell her that if she won't cooperate, we have enough to move forward with charges."

Charges?

The word sent icicles shooting through my veins.

He didn't wait for me to respond. He led me down a hallway to another room with an identical table and chairs.

Lila was inside.

She was still wearing the clothes from yesterday. Her head was on the table, cradled in her arms. Her dark hair hung in messy waves around her face.

When the door clicked shut behind us, she looked up. Her eyes were bloodshot, her cheeks blotchy. She looked so much younger than her forty-six years.

"Mom," she whispered—just one small, broken word.

My heart cracked open.

I crossed the room in a heartbeat and folded her into my arms. Or tried to. Instead of collapsing against me, she stiffened, so I released her and pulled back.

For a long, aching moment, neither of us spoke.

"What's going on?" I asked as I settled into the seat across from her. "The detective said you won't talk to them."

She took a long, slow breath before she answered. "Why should I? They think I'm guilty."

"You don't know that," I said. "Just tell them what happened."

She shook her head. "I didn't do anything. I swear it."

"I know, honey." I tried to touch her hand. She let me, but just barely. "They just need to hear it from you."

Her lower lip trembled. She bit down hard to stop it. A second later, she said, "I can't."

"Why not?"

Her gaze darted to the corners of the room like she half-expected someone or something to step from the shadows.

I wanted to ask if it had anything to do with Saphira. Had she known about that poor phantom creature?

But I couldn't risk it.

Platt could be back any moment, or listening, for all I knew. And above everything else, we had to protect our supernatural community.

So instead, I asked the safest question I had.

"Do you have any idea who did poison Evangeline?"

Lila shook her head. "No. How would I? These are your friends, not mine."

She had a point. Still, I studied her face, searching for any sign of knowing anything that might help.

What I found instead was exhaustion, fear, and a muddle of emotions I couldn't begin to unwind.

"Lila," I begged, "do you remember anything? Did anything feel off?"

I thought she was about to say something when the door swung open, and Detective Platt barged back in with all the subtlety of a marching band. "Ms. Boudreaux," he said crisply, "I'm going to need you to wrap this up."

I squeezed Lila's hand—a promise that this conversation wasn't over.

Not even close.

Chapter 8

Moral Support

As I LEFT THE police station, all I wanted to do was crawl back into bed and pull the covers over my head.

Kheppy, curled in a tight ball on the passenger seat, lifted her head just long enough to give me a pointed look as I started the engine. "You seem upset," she murmured, her silver whiskers twitching. "Are we going home?"

"I wish. I still have a business to run," I said, rubbing circles at my left temple as the Boo-tique loomed over my thoughts.

If I didn't get my Thanksgiving-friendly merchandise front and center today, I'd miss the last-minute shoppers, and those were the Boo-tique's bread and butter. Those were my people.

As I rolled down the familiar street, looking for a place to park, I noticed Sissy in the shop's window, wading through orange tissue paper and a cheerful pile of plush pumpkins from the new shipment. She'd propped a wooden "Give Thanks (for Candy)" sign beside them, which felt very on-brand.

And there, next to the display, stood Petunia—the mannequin I'd dressed as a blue-haired witch for the Halloween season.

Only Petunia didn't look particularly witchy at the moment. Sissy had tied a bright orange apron around her waist, patterned with acorns and leaves. She even held a faux casserole dish in her hands, which looked suspiciously like a tabletop cauldron spray-painted forest green.

Had Sissy done all that on her own? She must have, because I hadn't. That girl really was a treasure.

Next to me, Kheppy rose on her hind legs and pressed her nose to the glass. "Your shop sprite appears to have things under control."

I pulled into a parking spot half a block away and watched. I had to agree with Kheppy. Sissy moved cheerfully around the display, her ginger-blond hair bouncing as she worked, oblivious to me observing from afar because I didn't trust myself to walk inside without falling apart.

I picked up my phone and tapped her name.

She pulled her phone from her shop apron pocket and answered.

"Boo? Everything okay?" Her voice carried her usual youthful energy, threaded with just enough concern to remind me I wasn't fooling anyone these days.

"Absolutely." I watched her through the windshield as she straightened a stack of miniature hay bales. "Could you do me a favor and move the Thanksgiving merchandise to the front? Delphine needs me at home for something."

Not exactly true. But it sounded like a reasonable excuse.

Sissy planted her hands on her hips and eyed the display. "Sure! I'm almost done with the window," she said. "Petunia has a whole new outfit. I think you'll like it."

"It looks—" Oops. I nearly gave myself away. "I'm sure it looks great. I've been meaning to change it myself."

"How's Lila?" she asked, softening immediately. "Have you seen her?"

"She's fine." The words nearly caught in my throat.

Kheppy's tail brushed against my elbow, a soft, grounding touch. She didn't say anything. She didn't need to. I could hear the strain in my own voice, so I was certain Sissy could too.

"Okay," Sissy said after a brief pause. "Anything I can do to help?"

All I wanted to do was reach across the street and pull that sweet girl into a bear hug. I had to swallow hard before I could answer. "You're already doing it, doll. Thank you for handling the shop. Call if you need anything. Anything at all, you hear me?"

"I will." Her tone brightened again. "The Boo-tique is safe with me."

"I know it is," I said and forced myself to hang up.

I lingered another heartbeat as she turned back to Petunia and fussed with the apron strings. Then I put the car in gear and pulled away. The sight of my little storefront dressed for Thanksgiving should have made me happy. Instead, my heart felt like it was being yanked out of my chest.

The drive home through the canyon felt shorter than usual, probably because my brain kept grinding through the moments leading up to Evangeline's death.

But as I turned onto our lane, something unusual snapped me back to the present.

The garden witches' vehicles were parked in front of the house.

I slowed. "What do you suppose that's about?"

Kheppy rose to see what I meant. "Delphine didn't mention she was expecting visitors."

"No, she didn't," I whispered. "But I can't say I'm surprised."

These weren't just visitors. Our little flower-power coterie was practically family.

When I opened the front door, all three of them were there: Jemma, Opal, and Willa—sitting in the front room like they'd been there a while.

Delphine emerged from the kitchen carrying a plate of leftover shortbread and lemon bars.

"Oh, good," Delphine breathed, her shoulders easing. "You're here."

I smiled at the earnest faces looking back at me, trying not to look as baffled as I felt by their presence. After a moment, I gave up and told the truth.

"Am I interrupting?" I asked. "Or did I forget something?"

Opal shook her head, her black bob brushing over her shoulders. "We just came by to see if there was anything we could do to help."

"We know what a difficult time this must be," Jemma added, looking more well-rested than she had the day before.

From the way she said it, it was clear someone had already filled her in on what she'd missed.

Willa leaned forward, her warm brown eyes holding something that made my throat tighten, a blend of concern and unmistakable, motherly compassion.

"We wanted to offer our support," she said quietly. "For you and Lila."

"Moral support," Opal added.

"Whatever's needed," Jemma chimed in, ever the enthusiastic one.

I swallowed hard, caught off guard by the sudden wave of gratitude.

"You didn't have to do that."

"Of course we did," Jemma said. "You'd do the same for any of us."

Kheppy hopped into the empty chair beside me and tucked her paws neatly beneath her.

"They're your friends," she said with quiet resolve. "Let them help."

The simple generosity of it nearly undid me.

"Delphine has been trying to catch us up," Willa said. "But I think we should hear it from you."

"Right," I said. "Then I'm going to need tea first."

My sister handed me a cup and filled it from the nearby teapot. I sank into a chair while she passed around a platter of treats.

For a moment, it all felt so normal, so comfortingly ordinary.

Then my mind caught up and reminded me that nothing about today was normal. Across town, my daughter was still sitting in a police station.

The questions came next.

How was Lila? When would she be coming home? Was I eating? Sleeping?

That last one earned a rueful laugh. As it turned out, none of us had slept at all.

I answered what I could, choosing my words carefully, doing my best not to come undone.

Through it all, I kept finding my gaze drawn to Willa.

Calm. Controlled. Focused.

And something else. Something that was still bothering me from earlier.

Claire's voice drifted back to me, her quiet admission that she and Willa shared a history I'd never heard about.

I studied Willa. There was nothing overtly secretive about her manner, yet something behind her eyes struck me as guarded in a way it never had before.

But I wasn't going to blurt out Claire's confession in front of everyone. This wasn't the time or place. Not with my nerves hanging by a thread and my daughter in police custody.

When there was a lull, Willa rose and brushed her palms lightly along her pants. She turned to Delphine and asked, "May I trouble you for a few sprigs of lavender to take home?"

"Of course. I can pull some from a bundle I'm drying in the pantry." My sister set down her cup.

Willa waved her back. "I'd prefer fresh sprigs from the garden, if you don't mind. I could use the exercise."

Delphine leaned back. "In that case, help yourself. Take as much as you'd like."

Willa thanked her and slipped out the kitchen door.

I watched it shut behind her.

My moment.

I rose abruptly and set down my tea.

"I'm going out too," I said. "I could use some fresh air."

Delphine raised a brow. "You okay?"

"Peachy," I answered. Too fast. Too eager. Definitely suspicious.

My sister gave me a look that said *I know you're lying*.

And she was right. I was.

Chapter 9

Lavender

WILLA WAS BENT OVER a lavender bush with a pair of gardening shears gleaming in her hand when I stepped out of the kitchen onto the back porch.

For a moment, the sun broke through the gray morning clouds and caught the metal. It sent a shiver down my spine. Not that I actually thought Willa might attack me with those shears, but after the past couple of days, I was simply on edge.

"Need any help?" I called out as I approached her.

Willa straightened and squinted at me. "You really here to help or for something else?" That look told me she knew it was something else.

"Wanted some air," I said, looking over her shoulder at the lavender bush and darker clouds rolling from the shore. "But I'm happy to help."

"Good," she said. "I could use a steadier pair of hands." She handed me the shears and pointed to a few more pretty stems.

I crouched to snip them. "It means a lot that you came today," I said. "The others too. Thank you."

"Don't be silly," she replied, turning her attention to another cluster a few feet away. "We're always here for you. We're here for each other. That's part of the deal, right? We stick together, no matter what. Maybe you should tell me what's really on your mind. Is it Lila?"

I sighed. It probably should have been Lila. My daughter should have been my top concern, not running after clues that might be nothing more than figments of my imagination. "It's Claire."

"Oh," she said. "What about her?"

"I visited her today to apologize for last night's troubles, and she mentioned you. How close you two were." I watched Willa's face for her reaction. Surprise? Guilt? I saw nothing at all. "She's been here a few years now," I continued. "Why didn't you ever mention your connection?"

My friend seemed to be studying the stem between her fingers, but I knew she was stalling. Finally, she said, "I didn't tell anyone because I didn't think it was my place. Claire came here to make a fresh start. When she arrived, she asked me to keep our former association and her past quiet, so I honored that."

Something in my chest shifted. I knew something about fresh starts myself. I'd once left Laguna Bay for New Orleans chasing one. It hadn't lasted long—but I knew how fragile those first steps could be.

"I get it," I said.

Willa pointed out another few sprigs of lavender for me to clip. After I added them to the basket, she continued down the path with her usual easy confidence.

Meanwhile, my insides were in full-tilt upheaval, and I had no doubt it showed on my face. I tried to match her pace, hoping a little of that calm composure might rub off on me—treating it like a quiet lesson rather than something forever out of reach.

"That said, I have been looking out for her," she admitted. "A little. She's had some bumps in the road, but nothing that should concern you." She paused, then added more pointedly, "You've met her. You know she's not capable of anything horrible."

Claire's cheerful face flashed through my mind. Was she capable of murder? I had to admit, I couldn't see it. My gut resisted the idea immediately. Claire didn't feel like a killer. But instinct wasn't evidence, and I couldn't afford to ignore the facts.

"But if it wasn't Claire," I said, "then who?"

Willa hesitated.

She opened her mouth. Closed it again.

"Oh no," I said, fearing what that silence could mean. "You can't hold back now. You've been thinking about it, haven't you?"

She lowered her voice, like Delphine and the others might overhear, but I'd made sure to close the back door securely. "I saw something last night. Before Evangeline collapsed. The council elders were arguing behind the greenhouse when they thought no one else was around."

A chill crawled up my arms. Laguna Bay's supernatural elders—Cornelia, Howard, and Neal—rarely argued.

"Arguing about what?" I asked.

"I don't know. They clammed up the second they saw me."

The creak of the kitty door opening and closing behind us made me turn.

Kheppy padded out. As she approached, she regarded us with a wary expression. "You're up to something," she purred.

Willa bent down to stroke her back. "How wise you are, little one." She cocked her head. "Speaking of which, has Boo asked you what *you* think happened to Evangeline? Your feline instincts would have picked up something, I'm sure."

Kheppy sat and licked her paw. "Quite true. But I wasn't in the yard when Evangeline collapsed. I was inside asleep."

Willa stood. "That's a shame. There is something else I remember," she added. "Right after the argument, Cornelia seemed especially out of sorts. That isn't like her."

No, it wasn't.

"What about Howard and Neal?" I asked.

"Howard was upset, but Neal?" She gave me a look that said what we both knew. Nothing ever upset Neal.

I felt my jaw tighten. "Every time something goes wrong in this town, Cornelia seems to be right in the middle of it."

Kheppy swished her tail. "Vampires are control freaks," she said. "They can't help themselves."

"There may be some truth to that," I muttered.

Cornelia loved control—and Evangeline had threatened the town's very existence.

"It's not proof of anything," Willa warned gently as she gathered her lavender sprigs. "But the timing was strange."

I couldn't argue.

The knot in my stomach tightened. Not even the lavender's clean, floral scent, normally so calming, eased that tension.

I bent down and stroked Kheppy's head. "Do you have any thoughts about what the elders were fighting about?"

Kheppy pressed into my touch. "No, but you could try asking them about it."

I was thinking the same thing.

"If you're going to do that, you should probably start with Howard," Willa said. "He likes you."

"He tolerates me," I corrected.

Kheppy lifted her whiskers. "Neal tolerates you too."

"Yes, I suppose he does," I said.

Howard and Neal might tolerate me, but no matter how hard I tried to focus elsewhere, Cornelia kept slipping back into the picture.

Willa straightened again, brushing dirt from her hands. "Do we need a plan?"

"I have one," I said. "I know who I need to see."

A breeze stirred the lavender. Maybe it was just my nerves—or maybe it was a warning. Either way, Cornelia was my next stop.

Chapter 10

Message Received

I WAS ON MY way to the *Laguna Bay Gazette* when I took a detour past the Boo-tique for the second time that morning. I couldn't help myself. I wanted to make sure Sissy was all right. If I were being honest, a sliver of guilt came with it too, for leaving the shop in her hands.

Of course, she was fine. More than fine. She was still stationed in the front window, a force of nature wrapped in blush-pink overalls.

She'd finished redecorating the display with Petunia—my blue-haired mannequin, now sporting an adorable autumn apron—and had moved on to polishing the glass from the inside with a spray bottle and rag.

I hadn't asked Sissy to do any of that.

A warm pang bloomed in my chest. I'd been so wrapped up in the murder investigation and the constant knot of worry about Lila that I'd barely remembered I had a shop. And yet there Sissy was—keeping it running and making it beautiful without being asked.

If I made it through this murder mess without collapsing into a puddle of stress, I was going to give that kid a raise. Or a promotion. Maybe both. Plus a cake.

I didn't have time to stop, but I caught her eye when she glanced up. She waved brightly, her grin wide and proud. I waved back and drove on.

A few more blocks brought me to the *Gazette*, a modest storefront with faded blue trim and a news rack out front. As I stepped out of my Karmann Ghia, I ran my fingers through my hair, as if that might defend my blue waves from the damage the damp morning was doing.

It didn't. But I felt a little better, and that would have to be enough.

Inside, the room hummed with the *rat-a-tat-tat* of keyboards as reporters and clerks stared into their screens behind the glass wall.

A young man sat at the reception desk. It was someone I didn't recognize. Early twenties, maybe. Clean-cut, in a button-down shirt.

He perked up when he saw me.

"Hi," I said, striking what I hoped was a friendly tone. "I'd like to speak with Cornelia."

His eyebrows lifted slightly. "Do you have an appointment with Ms. Sloane?"

"No, but it's important."

He gave a small, uncertain nod as if he were about to give me the brush-off.

Before he could, Zelda Harcourt—Cornelia's wildly ambitious assistant with even wilder curls—poked her head around the corner.

Her expression hardened the instant she saw me. "What do you want, Ms. Boudreaux?"

There it was. Classic *Gazette* hospitality.

Zelda looked at me with a wary squint that made me wonder how much she remembered of our last encounter with Kheppy's mesmerizing charm, including her enthusiastic request for Cornelia to turn her into a vampire.

I played it cool. Just in case.

"It's private," I said.

Zelda hesitated. I saw something flash in her eyes behind her thick glasses. Uncertainty? Maybe even fear. But after a beat, she relented.

"You can have a seat. I'll see if she has time to see you."

She vanished again.

I lowered myself into one of the stiff lobby chairs. My heart tapped faster in my chest. I hated this part, the waiting, the wondering, the knowledge that Cornelia seemed to have a talent for finding the soft spots in people and poking them with her perfectly manicured nails.

Zelda reappeared a few minutes later.

"Cornelia will see you," Zelda said flatly.

I followed her down the hallway, each step clicking faintly against the tile. Behind us, the newsroom buzzed with its usual controlled chaos—phone conversations drifting in and out, keyboards clattering like impatient rain, printers spitting out fresh pages. Even the police scanner murmured softly in the background.

Zelda opened the frosted-glass door of the corner office with Cornelia's name etched in clean, serif letters. "Here she is," she said, then stalked away, leaving the door propped open.

I walked in to find Cornelia standing behind her white acrylic desk like she was expecting a fight. Her pale blond hair pulled into a sleek twist, her blouse crisply pressed, and her lips tucked into something only a nudge away from a frown.

She didn't bother greeting me.

"I don't have a lot of time, Boo, so tell me what you want," she said.

It was about as close as Cornelia ever came to small talk.

"Fine. I'll make it quick." I looked at her desk, at her bookshelf, at the window—anywhere but those icy blue eyes of hers. I wouldn't allow her to work one of her vampire glamours on me. "Why were you arguing with Howard and Neal at the party yesterday?"

Cornelia's perfect brows arched upward with irritation. "Who said we were arguing?"

"You're denying it?" I asked.

Her eyes narrowed to slits. "Close the door," she ordered.

I did.

She crossed her arms and leaned back against her credenza with measured ease.

"Council business is not your business, Boo," she said. "It was a private conversation, and that's all you need to know."

"You're right." I pulled out my phone. "If you'd rather have the police involved, let's invite Detective Platt over. I didn't think you'd want that, given how much you value your privacy, but I guess I was wrong."

Cornelia tipped her head back and groaned. "It's not your concern."

"It is when someone ends up dead in my backyard," I said.

"It's completely unrelated."

"I'm supposed to take your word for that?" I asked.

Her gaze cooled. "Yes, Boo. You are. Or are you suggesting I had something to do with Evangeline's death?"

I stiffened and looked away.

She came around the side of the desk, each movement smooth and deliberate. "I'm getting a little tired of you accusing me every time someone drops dead around here."

I opened my mouth, but she cut me off.

"You should be thanking me," she continued. "I have it on good authority that your daughter is sitting at the police station as the number-one suspect in this case. There could have been a story in today's paper saying exactly that, but I made sure that didn't happen. You're welcome."

I sucked in a sharp breath.

"I understand your situation," she said, unbothered. "But don't let your motherly instincts cloud your judgment. Are you sure—*really sure*—Lila is so innocent?"

I froze.

The question didn't just hit. It slammed into me and knocked the air from my lungs.

"That's a low blow," I said, my voice thinner than I wanted.

Cornelia glared at me.

Before I could recover enough to speak again, the door swung open.

Zelda stuck her head inside. "Sorry to interrupt, but the mayor-elect is on the line."

Cornelia rolled her eyes. "He won't even be sworn in until next week, and he's already called me more times today than the last mayor called in a month."

Zelda hesitated. "Should I—"

"Tell him to hold on to his chef's coat," Cornelia muttered, referring to Glen Phan's propensity for wearing chef whites at Beachside Café even though he hadn't worked in the kitchen in years. Then she gave me a long, meaningful look. "We're done here."

Message received.

I stepped into the hallway after Zelda and pulled Cornelia's office door shut behind me.

As I left, I heard Cornelia mutter, "Such a pain in the—"

The last word was lost behind the click of the latch, but I didn't need to hear it to get the gist. What I didn't know was whether she was referring to Chef—now soon to be Mayor—Glen or me.

Probably for the best.

I moved through the hallway in a kind of fog, every step heavy. My mind spun like a cart with a loose wheel.

Are you sure—really sure—Lila is innocent?

When I reached the lobby, I brushed past the new guy without a word and stepped outside.

The morning clouds felt darker. Heavier. A lone gull screeched overhead, raspy and grating. A delivery truck rumbled by, releasing a nauseating cloud of diesel.

My feet carried me across the street automatically. I didn't think. I couldn't.

I'd refused to consider even the remote possibility that Lila could have been involved. That she could have poisoned Evangeline even by accident.

But Cornelia's words stuck like burrs under my skin.

Had I been fooling myself?

That was the awful truth—I didn't know.

I reached my car, opened the door mechanically, and sank into the seat. I didn't start the engine. Didn't even grab the wheel. I just sat. Hands in my lap. Heart unspooling.

I pressed the heel of my hand against my chest, trying to calm the ache. I whispered into the silence, "I can't lose her. Not again."

The words had barely left my mouth before the awful possibility took shape in my mind. Slowly at first, then with the terrifying clarity of a candle flame catching on dry kindling.

What if Cornelia was right? What if my running around, my questions and theories and frantic digging had been nothing more than a deliberate attempt to ignore what was right in front of me?

Had I blindfolded myself with hope?

A tremor rippled through me. For the first time since this nightmare began, I didn't know whether I was trying to uncover a murderer or trying to protect myself from a horrible truth.

I gripped the steering wheel, knuckles white, and stared blindly through the windshield.

I wasn't sure I was ready for the answer.

Not anymore.

Chapter 11

Tide Pools

THE GRAY CLOUDS LINGERING all morning had deepened into something ready to burst. Under normal circumstances, that would've concerned me, especially with my driver's window still stuck slightly open. One good downpour could wreak havoc on my beloved Karmann Ghia. But right then, the car was the least of my problems.

Fixing that stupid window climbed a few notches on my to-do list, but it could wait. What mattered was finding a little space—to breathe, to think—before the coil of nerves Cornelia had wrapped around me tightened any further and that sick feeling creeping in swallowed me whole.

There was one spot in Laguna Bay that reliably set me right. Somewhere I could pull myself together before I completely unraveled.

And if I was going to sort through the mess in my head, I'd need something warm and steady to anchor me. Tea had a way of doing that better than anything else.

So I drove straight to Beachside Café, letting muscle memory handle the steering while my thoughts continued their full-scale rebellion. The bell jingled as I stepped inside. I half expected to see Chef Glen behind the counter, but he must have been busy with mayor-elect duties. Instead, a young server greeted me with a bright smile and took my order—chamomile tea, extra hot, to go.

When she handed me the giant paper cup, I accepted it with both hands, eager for the heat to seep into my cold palms.

As I drove away, a single ray of sunshine broke through the overcast sky, sharp and sudden. I took it as a hopeful sign, and it must have worked. During the summer, street parking along the beach was practically a competitive sport. Drivers circled like hungry gulls, waiting for someone to give up a space. Today, though, the curbside spots were plentiful. I found one easily near the concrete staircase that led from the street to the sand below.

I got out, pulled on a purple cap—crocheted by Delphine last winter—and buttoned my denim jacket before making my way down.

The tide was low, leaving a long, winding stretch of sandy shore before I reached the exposed rocks, slick with seawater and dotted with little puddled worlds of their own.

The breeze bit at my cheeks as I stepped carefully between the tide pools, my tea in one hand and the other holding back my hair to keep the breeze from blowing it in my face.

When I reached my favorite shallow pool, I crouched and ran my fingers gently along its rim. A starfish clung to one side. Beside it, two silvery crabs wrestled over a scrap of seaweed, their legs skittering so fast they reminded me of typewriter keys.

I sipped my tea, and its warmth spread through my chest. Everything was slowing down, or maybe it was me.

It hit me then—in a soft, painful sweep—that I used to bring Lila here when she would visit during her breaks from school. She'd loved the tide pools, loved how alive they were. I could almost hear her excited gasp the first time she'd spotted a starfish.

The thought tugged at a thread inside me, unraveling something I'd tried so hard to keep together.

"Is this tide pool taken?"

At the sound of that familiar drawl, I smiled despite myself. I hadn't heard him follow me—not the boots on the rocks, not the low grunt as he navigated the crevices, not even the faint sigh when he stopped behind me. I'd been too lost in my memories to notice much of anything. It was his voice—deep and rich as melted butterscotch—that finally did it.

I turned with care so I wouldn't lose my footing.

Merle stood there with a hand on his cowboy hat so the gusty breeze wouldn't blow it away. His mocha-brown Western shirt looked too thin for the wind whipping off the water.

I shaded my eyes with the hand that had been holding back my hair. "What are you doing here?"

He shrugged. "I was finishing lunch at the café when you walked in. You looked a million miles away, and then I saw you heading this direction." He paused. "I know this is where you come to think, so... well, I figured you might need a friend."

I'd come here to be alone, but the moment he said it, I knew he was right. I did need a friend, or whatever we were now. The lines between us had blurred in the best and most confusing ways, and I was still a little fuzzy on what to call it. But considering the kisses we'd shared since deciding to give this romance thing another shot, we were definitely something more than just friends.

"So you followed me?" I asked.

His eyes crinkled at the corners. "I guess I did." He stepped closer, his boots scraping lightly against the stone. "Yesterday was pretty awful, and I know you're upset about Lila. I wanted to be sure you were all right."

A lump formed in my throat.

"The truth is," I said, staring down at that starfish like it might give me courage, "I don't know if I am."

He didn't rush me. Didn't fill the space with chatter. He just waited, giving me all the time I needed.

Another gust brushed past us, carrying the briny scent of waves and kelp. I wrapped my hands around the cup and took another sip.

"I've been going over everything," I said finally. "I've been so worried about protecting her that I think I blinded myself to the possibility that she may have been involved."

Merle's expression softened. "Come here," he whispered, opening his arms.

I stepped into his embrace like someone coming home. His chest was strong and solid, and I could smell the remnants of his pine-scented soap. The hug was gentle, just enough support without suffocating me.

I hadn't realized how badly I needed that hug.

"You really think Lila might have had something to do with it?" he asked against my hair.

A shiver traced its way down my spine. "I don't want to think it," I said, "but I don't know anymore. I suppose anyone can do anything, depending on the circumstances." I swallowed. "And she's been different since she came back."

"Different how?" he asked.

I'd known that question was coming, but I still didn't have a decent answer. "I don't know how to explain it. She used to be so full of life, and now..." I trailed off, searching for the right word. "Now she feels hollow."

I exhaled slowly. "I thought it was Evangeline. That woman kept such a tight grip on her. Maybe she broke something in her." My voice wobbled despite my best efforts. "I just don't know."

I lifted my gaze to his. "I need to see her again."

He pulled back enough to look at me. "You have good instincts. Always have. If that's what you need to do, you should do it."

"Yeah," I said as the idea took hold. "That's what I'm going to do,"

This time, I wasn't asking for permission.

This time, I'd already decided.

"I want to come with you."

His offer hit me with a strange mixture of comfort and hesitation. Merle was nothing if not loyal. But this wasn't his burden to carry.

"I appreciate that," I said, brushing my fingers along his arm. "But I need to do this alone."

His jaw shifted, the tiniest muscle working near the hinge. He didn't like it. Yet he understood.

He adjusted his hat. "All right. Let me know if you need me. Please."

"I will," I promised.

For a long moment, neither of us moved. Waves crashed against the rocks, and somewhere overhead a gull cried. The crabs I'd been watching earlier kept right on wrestling, as if nothing in the world had changed.

Merle broke the silence at last. "You know," he said, nudging a shell with the toe of his boot, "there's something you're forgetting."

"Oh?" I said, not looking at him.

"Evangeline may have kept Lila close in New Orleans," he went on, "but she's still your blood. No matter what that woman said or did, I don't believe your goodness skipped a generation." His voice dropped, the way it always did when he was trying to make a point. "People don't lose the light inside them."

His words landed hard. I wanted to believe him. Desperately.

"I hope you're right," I said.

"I usually am," he drawled.

I bumped his arm with my elbow, and he laughed, a warm, familiar sound that wrapped around me like one of Mama's old quilts. And for a brief moment there among the rocks and tide pools, with the salt breeze on my face and what was left of my tea cooling in my hands, the world didn't feel quite so heavy.

But the moment couldn't last.

"I should go," I said.

Merle nodded. "I'll walk you back."

We made our way out of the tide pools, stepping carefully around the slick rocks. When we reached the top of the cliffside staircase, I tossed my empty cup into the trash bin and turned back toward him.

"How about we grab lunch tomorrow," he said, "and you can fill me in."

It was his way of giving me space. "Lunch would be nice."

"Good." His blue eyes twinkled. "Don't worry, darlin'. You got this."

My breath hitched. He hadn't called me that in years. I wasn't sure what surprised me more. That he'd said it, or how much I'd missed it.

"Thank you," I said.

He tipped his hat and watched me climb into my car. I felt his gaze on me until I started the engine. Then he turned and headed toward his truck.

I sat for a moment, gripping the steering wheel. This time not in panic, but with purpose. The clouds thinned just enough for light to break through again. A long shiver passed through me, but it wasn't fear.

Not this time.

It was time to hear the truth from my daughter's own lips, and no police clerk or even Detective Platt was going to stop me.

Chapter 12

Coming Home

As I DROVE FROM the tide pools back to the police station, the sky deepened to a gunmetal gray, an unflattering shade that matched my mood a little too closely.

The same clerk was still behind the counter in the otherwise empty lobby. He looked up, recognized me, and stiffened ever so slightly.

"Back so soon?" he asked, forcing a strained smile.

"I want to see my daughter." My voice sounded harsher than I'd intended. "Lila Sage."

He glanced at his clipboard. "I'll have to get Detective Platt."

Of course. The thorn in my side. Or maybe it was the other way around.

While I waited, I hugged myself against the cold air that drifted in every time the doors opened and wondered why it was taking so long.

Just when I was about to ring the silver bell on the clerk's desk to get someone's attention, Detective Platt appeared from the back hallway. His shirt had picked up a few more wrinkles and another coffee stain.

"Ms. Boudreaux," he said, not unkindly. "Could I have a word?"

I steeled myself. "I'd like to speak to Lila first."

"We were actually about to call you," he said.

Fear shot through me. "Why? Has something happened to her?"

"We're releasing her."

My heart jumped into my throat. "You are?"

That was good news. Great news, even. So why did he look like he'd just taken a long swig of curdled milk?

I tried to focus on what mattered. "She's free to go?"

"Yes," he said, then added, "for now."

My stomach clenched. "What does that mean?"

"It means we aren't pressing charges at this time, but we've asked her to stay in town while the investigation continues."

"Does that mean you've got another suspect?" I asked.

He gave me a thin, practiced smile. "It means she's still refusing to cooperate. And without charges, we can't hold her. But new evidence is pushing the investigation in a different direction."

"Is she still a suspect?" I asked.

He wagged a finger at me. "Let's call her a person of interest. Would you like to see her now?"

"Of course," I said, and bit my tongue so I wouldn't add anything snide.

I followed him through a small hallway off the lobby. Lila was in another interview room. Her shoulders hunched, and her hair tangled from running her fingers through it.

When she saw me, she pushed herself to her feet—or tried to—before swaying, sinking back down, and dropping her head into her hands.

I moved toward her, every maternal instinct screaming, but I stopped short when she didn't lift her head. I rested a hand between her shoulder blades instead.

"You're coming home," I whispered. "Soon."

She nodded, but she didn't look at me.

"They think—" Her voice shook. "They still think I did it."

"No, honey," I said, maybe too quickly. "No one thinks that."

A lie. A hope. A promise. Maybe all three.

Whatever resolve I'd walked in with—to confront her, to seek the truth—evaporated on the spot. I didn't want answers. I wanted to protect her. I wanted to plant myself squarely between her and anything that might hurt her, logic be damned.

Lila sat there, trembling and guarded. I'd tried to tell myself it was that we were rusty, out of practice at being mother and daughter in the same room.

But this was something else.

She was different. More meek. Timid, even.

Had Evangeline done that to her?

Detective Platt cleared his throat. "Whenever you're ready."

Lila and I walked out of the station together. I helped her into the car and drove home, keeping one eye on the road and the other on her as she stared out the window with the distant look of someone trying to wake from a nightmare she couldn't escape.

As we motored through town, I tried to bridge the distance, commenting on the darkening clouds, asking if the seat was comfortable, offering to turn up the heater.

Lila answered each attempt with clipped, one-word replies, eyes fixed straight ahead.

When we pulled into the driveway, the house lights were already on, glowing warmly against the overcast sky. Delphine's car was there—along with every one of our garden witch pals' vehicles.

As we walked up the path, I asked Lila if she was hungry.

"I just want to lie down."

"Sure." I told myself not to take it personally, but it still felt like a rejection. "My room's all fixed up for you."

When we reached the porch, I paused. "Are you ready for this?"

Was I?

She nodded, so I opened the front door and did my best to body-block her from her aunt and the others, whose eager welcome was well-intentioned but came on like a friendly ambush.

Lila smiled, said the right things, and took it all in stride. But at the first opportunity, she excused herself and disappeared down the hall.

The bedroom door clicked shut.

The others fussed, then drifted back into conversation about the neighbor who'd stopped by for more of Delphine's tea. Apparently, she couldn't remember the last time she'd slept so well.

Delphine had promised to send over another batch, which—once the woman left—had set off an earnest debate about sharing charmed concoctions with a normie.

While they wrestled with that question, I struggled with one of my own: Was Lila involved in Evangeline's death?

It settled over me, heavy and unmoving, darker than the clouds piling up outside.

Delphine was working on dinner, standing by the stove with Willa and Jemma, sitting at the table nearby. Kheppy kept them company from her spot on the armchair.

Suddenly, their silence was deafening. Every eye was on me.

"Did I miss something?" I half-chuckled, trying to lighten the mood.

It didn't work.

Willa sat frozen at the table, sorting through bundles of lavender and rosemary, tying off the stems for drying. Jemma worked beside her, checking each bunch and stripping away any wilted or yellowing sprigs. Kheppy sat between them, tail curled neatly, her gaze fixed on me in her inscrutable way.

Delphine looked up from her stock pot. "Lila seems a little out of sorts? Is she all right?"

"Just tired, I think," I said, pulling a mug down from the cupboard and filling it from the teapot on the counter. "They aren't charging her, so that's a relief. Where's Opal?"

It seemed strange to be missing one of our gardening squad.

"She had to pick up her granddaughter from school," Jemma said as she tossed a wilted stem.

I glanced at the clock. Was it two-thirty already? The day was flying by.

"Do they have any details on the poison that killed Evangeline yet?" Jemma asked.

"The detective didn't say," I said.

"But he did say they were doing more tests. So, it was definitely poison, right?" Delphine asked.

"You know as much as I do," I said. "The detective didn't exactly share his case file with me."

"Maybe Merle could find out," Kheppy added.

I went to the armchair and plopped down beside her. "Maybe, but I can't ask him to do that."

"Why not?" Jemma asked. The way the others watched me, I knew they were wondering too.

I rubbed my forehead. "It feels wrong." I ran my hand down Kheppy's back. "Look, I don't think the case file is going to help anyway. Someone poisoned Evangeline at the party, and my guess is it was someone who was close enough to act without being noticed. We just need to figure out who it was."

I'd been inching closer to that idea for the past hour. If Lila had done it, I told myself I'd know it. I'd feel it. She couldn't be the killer because she was too broken to do something like that.

Willa watched me. "You should let this go. Let the police do their jobs."

I sipped the tea. "I can't. They move too slowly. They could be poking around our business for weeks, and who knows what they might uncover while they're asking and following people around? If we can figure it out on our own, maybe we can minimize the damage. We need to at least try, for the community's sake."

It wasn't a popular opinion. Delphine opened her mouth twice to argue with me, but shut it again without saying a word.

Willa was the first to speak. "I'm afraid you're right. But I'm also afraid of where this could lead."

It was my fear as well. Cornelia had done a good job distracting me, but now that Lila was home and out of the police crosshairs—at least for now—that argument between the council elders was once again foremost on my mind.

"I went to see Cornelia before I saw Lila," I said as I stared at my cup. "I asked her what she was arguing about with Howard and Neal."

"What did she say?" Willa asked.

"She wouldn't tell me," I said.

Willa huffed. "That's no surprise."

"I suppose not," I said. "But they have the most to lose if the High Council revokes Laguna Bay's charter."

"If you think about it," Jemma said, "one of them has more to lose than the others."

"Neal," Delphine whispered like a lightbulb went off in that beautiful brain of hers. "If Laguna Bay loses the High Council's protection, where would the merfolk go?"

Willa sighed. "We're the only certified seaside sanctuary on the West Coast."

Jemma frowned. "Evangeline's vendetta could have destroyed his community."

No one answered right away.

I held up a hand. "Let's not jump to conclusions." I drew in a slow breath, trying to still the swirl in my head. "Neal may have a motive, but c'mon—this is Neal we're talking about. I can't picture him hurting anyone. Can you?"

"Maybe not on purpose," Jemma said. "But desperate times..."

Kheppy's ear pulled back. "Was he desperate?"

"I suppose that's what we need to find out," I said, pushing myself to my feet. "Before this goes any further."

Everyone nodded.

But as I stood there, my gaze drifting down the hallway toward Lila's borrowed room, a tight ache twisted inside me.

Something felt wrong.

I believed my daughter, but I didn't have proof to back it up.

Then a memory surfaced. Lila's expression had hardened as Evangeline whispered to her moments before she collapsed. That flash of anger.

At the time, I'd pushed it aside. Now it came rushing back.

Rain tapped at the kitchen window, soft at first, then steadily more insistent. I listened, suspended between relief and dread, grateful that Lila was back under my roof and haunted by the certainty that someone in our supernatural family had already crossed a deadly line and might get away with it.

Chapter 13

Hot Seat

I'D BEEN PACING FOR ten—maybe fifteen—minutes when Delphine peeked into the living room for the second time, clearly wondering why I was procrastinating.

I took out my phone—again—and stared at Neal Glory's number.

"What's taking you so long?" Delphine asked from the kitchen, where she was camped out with Jemma and Willa.

"I'm thinking," I said, which was only half true.

"Just make the call," she urged.

"It's only hair," Kheppy added. "If he ruins it, it'll grow back."

"Is that supposed to be reassuring?" I asked. "Because it isn't."

Delphine rolled her eyes. "Boo, the best way to get Neal's attention is from his salon chair. Do you want one of us to do it instead?"

And admit defeat? Never.

"I'll do it," I said. "I just need a cover story. He knows I always color my own hair, and that you trim it. How do I explain suddenly needing his help now?"

"Pretend your roots are driving you crazy and you don't have time to fix them before Thanksgiving," Willa suggested.

"They *are* driving me crazy," I muttered, and the holiday was only a few days away.

But that wasn't the point. Not exactly.

What was really bothering me was that Neal—the council elder representing the merfolk—had no concept of personal boundaries when it came to hair. Every time he saw me, it was, "Boo, my dear, let me tame those curls!" Or "Come see me, sweetheart—let's weave some texture into that delicious blue hair."

Hard pass.

But today, I needed him to talk. I needed to know what he, Cornelia, and Howard had been arguing about at the party, and whether he had taken Evangeline's crusade against Laguna Bay personally.

With a deep breath, I hit *Call*.

Jemma folded her arms. "No way he has time. I had to book my appointment two months in advance."

"She won't know if she doesn't try," Willa offered.

The phone rang once.

Twice.

In the middle of the third, Neal's voice burst through the speaker like confetti from a cannon. "Laguna Spa and Salon, Neal Glory speaking. How may I brighten your day?"

It took every ounce of willpower I had not to hang up. "Hi Neal," I said. "It's Boo."

There was a sharp intake of breath.

"Finally!" he gushed. "You're calling about your roots, aren't you?"

I winced. If the others hadn't been watching me so closely, I would have ended the call right there.

"How did you know?" I asked slowly. "You wouldn't happen to have any time today, would you?"

Dead silence.

Then—

"For you, love? My schedule is always open. Come now. This instant."

I stuttered. "Really? Are you sure?"

"Boo," he said dramatically, "I've been waiting years for this moment."

I hung up, stunned.

"Congratulations," Kheppy said, "Apparently you are a VIP. Very Much In Need of Primping."

"Wouldn't that be a VMINP?" I growled back.

"*C'est la Veep*," she said with a nonchalant grin and sauntered away before I could correct her. Again.

Honestly, Kheppy's mangled phrases were the least of my worries. I groaned and grabbed my purse. "If I'm not back in two hours, send a rescue team."

"Will do," Delphine said, sucking in her cheeks as she tried—unsuccessfully—to hide her amusement.

"Good luck," Willa added, with the same smirk.

Outside, the rain was still coming down in a steady drizzle, so I pulled up my hood and taped plastic wrap over the inside of my temperamental car window with thick shipping tape, a makeshift weatherproofing solution that relied heavily on optimism and denial.

The entire drive to the salon, I rehearsed what I could say to get one of the sweetest men on the planet to give up information on what he and the other council elders had been arguing about, and whether he had a motive for murder.

All the while, doubt kept needling at me. Was he even capable of hurting another creature?

I reminded myself that desperation could make people do dangerous things, especially when a whole community was at stake.

As I pulled into an open parking spot near the salon's beachfront location, I still wasn't sure how to raise the issue, and it dawned on me my plan had another flaw. The Laguna Spa and Salon catered to a certain class of clientele... and I wasn't it.

Despite my misgivings, I stepped inside and was immediately enveloped in warm, fragrant air as soft harp music filled the space. Plush ivory chairs crowded the waiting area, looking like a flock of fancy marshmallows gathered around a glass-topped coffee table no one seemed brave enough to touch.

A young woman at the desk flashed me her impossibly white teeth. "Welcome! Do you have an appointment?"

"I think so," I said. "With Neal."

Her perfectly arched eyebrows shot up. "You must be Ms. Boudreaux. Come right this way. He's expecting you."

I had no doubt he was.

She led me past a nail station and massage rooms. As we entered the salon area, Neal stood out like a vibrant tropical bird among run-of-the-mill pigeons.

He was wearing a turtleneck striped in bright coral, teal, and lemon yellow, and somehow, it worked.

"Boo!" He rushed over and air-kissed my cheeks. "You actually came! I knew you would!"

Did he? That tone suggested he'd had his doubts.

"Here I am," I said, pulling off my jacket. "Be gentle."

"I make no promises," he gushed as he guided me to his chair. "Sit, sit. Let me have a look."

I lowered myself onto the beige leather cushion and instantly regretted everything. The chair was too rigid. The lights were too bright. The giant mirror was too honest.

"So, you've been doing your own color," he said as he fluffed my hair with his fingertips. "But it isn't too bad."

Too bad? Oh boy. This really was a mistake.

"I like doing it myself," I said defensively.

"I know," he said pointedly. "And it works. Darling, it works."

I tried to recall the list of questions I'd planned to ask, but my mind suddenly went blank.

"So," he said as he wrapped a silky black cape around me. "You came for the roots, but how about adding a bit of *zhuzh*? A little teal, a little purple, just enough to give this masterpiece some dimension. Some texture. Or maybe we go full mermaid ombré."

"No mermaid ombré," I said.

"Subtle ombré?"

"No ombré."

He clicked his tongue. "You're no fun."

"I'm plenty of fun," I said. "But I like this shade, and I'd like to keep it."

He sighed—dramatically. "Fine. We'll start with a simple refresh. But one of these days, Boo Boudreaux, you must let me give you the full fantasy color treatment."

"Don't hold your breath," I said.

He cast a quick glance around the room to make sure no one was within earshot, then leaned close to my ear. With a sly smile, he hooked a finger under the collar of his turtleneck and tugged it enough to reveal four faint, almost invisible slits in his throat.

"Sweetheart," he murmured, "I'm a citizen of the sea. Holding my breath is my specialty."

I snorted.

And just like that, we settled into an easy rhythm—him working, and me trying not to claw my way out of the chair.

After he washed my hair and plopped me back on the seat, he asked casually, "So what brings you in today? Truly. You've never struck me as someone who frets over roots."

I forced my shoulders to remain relaxed. "It just seemed like it was time."

He paused. Then hummed thoughtfully. "Uh-huh."

Heat crept up the back of my neck.

"Well," I said, scrambling to redirect, "I also wanted to see how you've been. Since... you know."

His nimble fingers stilled. "The party," he said.

"Yes."

He resumed sectioning my hair and brushing color onto the strands. "Tragic. Absolutely tragic. That woman was, well, she was many things. It's just such a shame."

I swallowed. "Did you see anything unusual that night?"

He shook his head. "Only what everyone else saw, I suppose. People talking, people eating, people laughing." He smirked as if he were remembering something. "Howard bickering with that new woman... What's her name? Kelly? No, Claire. She's the one with the pet cemetery, right?"

I nodded. "You saw Howard arguing with her? What about?"

"Not arguing exactly. More like..." He frowned, searching for words. "He had that pinched, disapproving look. You know the one. He was saying something like, 'Don't do that here.'"

"What was she doing?" I asked.

"I don't know." He unclipped another section of hair and dabbed it with dye. "Besides, who wants to get in the middle of something like that?"

I made an agreeing murmur, but why hadn't she mentioned that when I'd talked to her?

"Did Howard say what it was about?" I asked.

"No, and I try to keep my nose out of those kinds of tiffs. Life's too short."

I nodded, but something about the way he dismissed it struck me as odd. I'd seen part of that exchange myself. I wish I'd paid closer attention because it took a lot to rankle Howard.

Neal dabbed color along my temples. "You look troubled. What is it?"

"I'm just surprised something like that happened the same day... you know," I said.

"The same day Evangeline met her untimely end?" he asked.

The way he said it—*untimely end*—made it sound so innocent, as if she'd simply slipped away. Not like someone had deliberately killed her. But over the past few months, I'd learned a few hard truths about murder and the people who commit it.

The one I couldn't shake was this: You never really know what a person is capable of.

"Yes," I whispered.

The rain outside picked up, tapping harder against the wide salon windows. The diffused gray light made the room feel cocooned, warmer and safer than it probably should have.

Neal continued applying the dye to my hair and wrapping it in foil. "I think about it, too, you know. Who could've done it."

"You do?" I perked again.

"Of course. Who wouldn't? As elders, we're supposed to act like everything is fine, but believe me. We worry about everything."

"Is that why the three of you were arguing at the party?" I asked.

That seemed to startle him. "Who told you we were arguing?"

I considered lying, but what was the point? "Willa saw you."

He nodded. "Like I said, sometimes the tension gets to be too much. We all want what's best for the community, but we don't always agree on what that looks like."

"Willa thought the merfolk might be upset that Evangeline's threats were endangering Laguna Bay's sanctuary status." I hoped she wouldn't mind that I was embellishing the facts to get to the truth.

His brow wrinkled. "We're not upset," he said. "Not about the sanctuary, anyway."

I backpedaled. "What will happen to your people if the High Council removes our protections?"

Silently, I added, *What will happen to you?*

Instead of looking guilty, he scoffed. "I'm not worried about the sea people losing this place. I'm more concerned about keeping them here."

He must have noticed my confusion.

"You haven't heard?" he asked. "A new sanctuary has applied for a charter on Hawaii's Big Island. Gorgeous coral reefs. Warm currents. A supernatural council without all the baggage." He heaved a dramatic sigh. "Honestly,

Boo, if I didn't love Laguna Bay so much, I'd be considering my own relocation."

That was the first I'd heard of the new sanctuary. "So, you aren't worried about Laguna Bay losing its charter?" I asked.

"I am," he said, "but not because it'll leave us homeless."

So, we'd had it all wrong. Neal wasn't desperate.

"Then what were the three of you arguing about?" I asked.

That easygoing smile vanished. His jaw tensed.

"Sorry, Boo, that's not for me to say," he said.

A knot formed low in my stomach.

Suddenly, his earlier remark about Howard telling Claire to back off floated back to me.

If Neal wasn't desperate...

If he wasn't afraid...

Maybe someone else was.

A chill slid down my arms, raising every tiny hair.

Was it Howard?

The thought made my breath catch.

Neal didn't notice. He was guiding me back to the sink for a rinse.

But my mind wasn't on my hair.

I almost asked him outright about Howard, but something told me Neal wouldn't betray another elder that easily.

As the water cascaded over my head and Neal's fingers massaged my scalp, I let this new information tumble through my thoughts. Then he took me back to his chair and turned his industrial-strength blow dryer on me. As he worked, my reflection stared back at me.

Howard had lived in Laguna Bay longer than almost anyone. If the sanctuary collapsed, he would lose more than just a title. He would lose the place he'd built his entire life around.

If anyone had something to lose...

If anyone felt cornered...

I didn't like the idea of accusing Howard of doing something terrible. Something unforgivable.

But someone had done it, and it seemed more than likely that it was someone who was trying to protect the community.

Who was more protective than Howard?

Rain streaked down the salon's windows in soft ribbons while the warm dryer roared around my head. The rush of hot air should have been soothing.

But inside me, nothing felt calm.

Because suddenly, I could see the shape of a possibility I'd been trying hard not to consider.

Lila wasn't the only one acting strange.

Howard had been acting strangely too.

Maybe it was time to take a closer look at the man whose psychic gifts I'd never fully understood, gifts he'd always kept tucked away like a family secret.

The dryer clicked off, and for a heartbeat the whole room seemed to hold still.

Neal spun me away from the mirror as he finished performing his stylist magic, then, grinning from ear to ear, he bent down and asked, "Are you ready for it?"

I tried to smile, but in the pit of my stomach, dread unfurled like smoke.

Neal was talking about my color, but I was already thinking ahead.

Because the next stop in my investigation was going to be more complicated than spending a couple of hours at the salon.

I needed to talk to Howard.

And I had a feeling that conversation would change everything.

Chapter 14

November Rain

THE MOMENT I STEPPED outside the salon, the light November rain became a downpour. My freshly trimmed and colored hair was tucked safely beneath my hood, but I still hunched my shoulders instinctively as I raced to my car.

Neal had hugged me and fussed over whether my new, brighter blue shade was "vibrant enough to match my spirit." Normally, I would've found his attention charming, but today? I was torn.

On the one hand, I was glad he didn't appear to have a motive to kill Evangeline. I didn't want him to be guilty.

But that also meant the trail I'd been following had suddenly gone cold.

As I opened my car door, I was relieved to find my Karmann Ghia's interior hadn't flooded. My makeshift window fix was holding, at least so far.

On the drive home, I found myself wondering if Neal had meant what he'd said about some of his people possibly relocating to the new Hawaiian sanctuary. I couldn't say I'd blame them—warm currents and coral reefs sounded pretty appealing—but Laguna Bay wouldn't be the same without them. Or Neal, if he chose to follow them there.

Was that what the council elders had been arguing about at the party? It seemed possible.

What stuck with me even more were the sharp words Neal said he'd overheard between Howard and Claire.

Howard didn't have Neal's gentle temperament. He was more practical, but I could count on one hand the times I'd seen him upset. Last night had been one of them. He'd seemed agitated. Annoyed. Maybe it had been more than that.

Neal had refused to elaborate—or had he? His reference to Howard's confrontation with Claire suddenly felt less like gossip and more like a clue.

I turned that over in my mind as I drove through the rain, the wipers swishing back and forth in a lazy, almost hypnotic rhythm. As the road curved and the canyon narrowed, my thoughts drifted back to the party—to the moments just before Evangeline collapsed.

I tried to recall exactly when Howard had become tense. But then we all had been to some extent. We'd all been on edge over the threat Evangeline posed to our community.

Still, by the time I pulled into my driveway, I knew I couldn't ignore the possibility Neal was hinting at something more.

I hurried inside and went straight to the kitchen, where Jemma was bundling fresh lavender, Delphine stood at the sink washing vegetables, and Willa trimmed dried rosemary. Kheppy sat on a stool, watching it all like a small but perky supervisor.

On the stove, something savory and delicious simmered in a stockpot.

My gaze shot toward the hallway. "Where's Lila?"

"Still sleeping," Delphine said without looking up. "I checked on her a few minutes ago."

My anxiety eased. "Good," I said and pushed my hood back, letting the kitchen light catch the freshly trimmed strands, the blue deeper and more vivid than before.

Four pairs of eyes shifted fully to me.

Delphine's mouth curved. "It looks good. Really good."

Jemma nodded. "Nice glow-up."

"Thank you," I said, then let the moment pass. "But, more importantly, Neal didn't do it. He's not the guy."

The room fell into a heavy silence.

"Are you sure?" Jemma asked carefully.

I slid into an empty chair. "He has no motive."

"Tell us what happened," Delphine said.

I rubbed my eyes and pinched the bridge of my nose. "Did you know a new sanctuary is seeking a charter in Hawaii and that they're actively recruiting our mer residents?"

"I'd heard a new charter might be in the works, but nothing concrete, and certainly not that they were going after our people. How rude," Delphine said.

"You knew about Hawaii and you didn't tell me?" I shot back.

"I thought you knew. It was in the minutes of the last Midnight Council. I thought everyone knew." She glanced at Jemma, whose gaze was locked on a lavender bundle in front of her.

When Delphine's gaze landed on Willa, the older woman sucked in a breath. "It has been discussed as a possibility," she said diplomatically.

"Am I the only one who didn't know?" I asked.

"You've been busy," my sister said.

She was being kind. I had been busy—with the Boo-tique, with whatever awkward limbo Merle and I were currently calling a relationship, and with my recent brushes with the law. Still, none of that was supposed to outrank protecting our community. And that meant knowing what was happening beyond Laguna Bay.

"So the mer people aren't desperate at all." I tipped my head back and sighed. "That feels like information you could've shared before I left."

The pot lid rattled, and Delphine hurried to check it. "I thought it was still in the planning stages," she said. "Did he tell you why the elders were arguing?"

"No. But he said Howard and Claire had words. Do any of you know anything about that?"

"That's curious," Willa murmured, her voice low and uncertain.

As Delphine stirred the pot, the rich scent of rosemary, sage, and thyme wafted through the room and reminded me how hungry I was.

"Did Neal say anything else?" Willa asked.

I shook my head. "He said he didn't want to get involved."

A round of quiet nods followed. No one seemed surprised.

"What if Howard's hiding something?" Delphine asked as she offered me a bowl of vegetable noodle soup, then handed similar bowls all around.

"I don't want to think that's a possibility, but I suppose we have to consider it," I admitted before tucking in.

Jemma grabbed a slice of crusty brown soda bread Delphine pulled from the oven and dipped it into her bowl. "He has been acting odd lately."

Willa leaned in, interest sharpening her gaze. "What do you mean, odd?"

"Before I left, I noticed he seemed on edge, more short-tempered than usual," Jemma said. "I assumed it was nerves. Maybe it was something else."

We all agreed Howard hadn't seemed like his usual jovial self, but who could blame him? It was a perfectly reasonable reaction to the awkward reality of rolling out the welcome mat for a woman with a vendetta against our community.

Wasn't it?

After a long silence, Jemma asked, "Do you think he's even capable of something like that? Of doing something so desperate?"

The five of us sat there, contemplating the question and coming to the same uncomfortable conclusion. Under the right circumstances, especially if he thought he was protecting the community, yes. He probably could.

Which meant Howard was no longer just a name on my suspect list. He was quickly rising to the top.

"Are you going to talk to him?" Jemma asked, looking at me.

"What's the point?" Willa snapped, surprising all of us. "This is Howard we're talking about. It's not like he'd confess just because Boo walks in and bats her eyelashes."

"Hey," I said, mildly offended. "I don't bat my eyelashes. Ever."

"You know what I mean," she grimaced. "He's not a talker. Not like Neal."

Delphine covered her stockpot and leaned against the counter, arms folded. "Willa's right. Howard is more the quiet type."

"So, you don't think I should talk to him?" I asked.

"Oh, you definitely should," Delphine corrected. "But you need a plan."

Jemma nodded. Willa appeared more dubious.

I stared into my soup, watching steam spiral in lazy curls. I'd always trusted Howard, but that didn't ease the gnawing feeling working its way through me.

"I'll go see him tomorrow," I said finally. "I'll ask his advice on how to handle the nosy neighbor now that she's so keen on Delphine's sleepy-time tea. See what he says."

"That's a good opener," Jemma said.

"Smart," Delphine added.

"Still dangerous," Willa muttered.

Kheppy glanced up at me. "Let me come with you."

I nodded. "Actually, I'd like that. Thank you."

Outside, the rain had picked up again, tapping insistently against the kitchen window like a heartbeat.

Kheppy curled up on my thighs, her purr low and comforting. I rested a hand on her back, letting the familiar warmth of her fur calm my nerves.

"What if I'm wrong?" I whispered to the room—but mostly to her.

She didn't answer right away. Her tail swayed once, twice, before she tucked herself even closer.

"What if you're right?" she murmured.

I stared out the window at the rain-blurred world beyond the glass.

That was the question pressing in. Because tomorrow, I'd either have an awkward conversation with a friend, or find out my instincts had failed me again.

Chapter 15

Television Glow

SOMETHING WOKE ME. NOT loud, but loud enough to slip into my dream and tug me awake like an insistent tap on the shoulder.

It took a moment to reorient myself. I'd been sleeping on the futon in Delphine's craft room since giving my bedroom to Lila. For a second I thought the rain was back, but the window was silent. Only moonlight brushed the glass.

Then it was there again. Faint, but unmistakably present.

I pushed myself up on my elbows.

"Kheppy?" I whispered.

The silver-gray lump beside me didn't move. Curled against my pillow, paws tucked beneath her chin, she breathed in the slow, even rhythm of deep slumber. Her whiskers twitched once, but that was it.

It hadn't been her.

I slid out of bed carefully, not wanting to wake my feline companion, and reached for my robe. The floor was cool against my bare feet, a sharp reminder that late November nights in Laguna Bay could still get chilly. I paused and listened again.

There it was—a soft rise and fall of sound, too indistinct to make out, but steady enough to be voices. Or maybe just one voice.

My pulse quickened. For half a second, I wondered if it might be an intruder.

Not tonight. I didn't have the energy for it.

Still, I slipped out of my bedroom and moved down the hallway. The sound grew louder, accompanied by a dim flicker along the walls. A muted bluish-white glow, then brighter, stretching across the living room floor in pale rectangular patches.

I exhaled as the pent-up tension eased.

Not an intruder. Just the television.

In the living room, Lila was lying on the couch, a blanket wrapped around her, the TV casting shifting shadows across her face. Something Victorian was playing—ruffled skirts and horse-drawn carriages. The volume had been turned down, but I'd recognize the familiar faces of the Toronto Constabulary's Station House No. Four anywhere.

My daughter glanced up when she noticed me. Her eyes were glassy, her hair rumpled. She sat up and fumbled for the remote.

"I'm sorry," she muttered, pressing the mute button. "I didn't mean to wake you."

"It's all right," I said, leaning against the doorframe. "I'm just not used to noise in the house." I tipped my chin toward the kitchen. "You slept through dinner. You must be starving. Can I fix you something?"

For a split second, she looked like she might smile. Then the wall came back down.

"I helped myself to some of Aunt Del's soup," she said. "I'm fine. I just didn't feel like sleeping anymore."

I should have felt completely at ease, but every time I looked at her, a prickle of guilt surfaced. We'd been apart for so long. I'd hoped this reunion would give us a chance to reconnect, yet even standing in the same room, it felt like we were miles apart.

And beneath it all lurked a thought I didn't want to face, that she was keeping secrets.

"How about tea?" I asked.

She hesitated, then nodded. "Yeah. Tea would be nice."

"Chamomile?"

"That's fine."

The warm scent of soup lingered in the kitchen as I filled the kettle and set it on the stove. When the water was ready, I steeped two bags of Delphine's chamomile blend and carried the mugs back to the living room.

I handed one to Lila and settled into the armchair.

For a while, we drank in silence while the detective on the television studied a clue beneath a streetlamp.

Lila finally spoke without looking at me.

"You don't think I had anything to do with Grand-mama's death, do you?"

My breath caught.

"Of course not," I said quickly.

She pulled the blanket up to her chin.

"I couldn't bear it if you did," she murmured.

"I don't," I said firmly.

The words came easily, but the twist in my gut told a different story. I didn't want to believe she could be involved.

But I'd learned the hard way that wanting something didn't always make it true.

And lately it seemed like everyone around me was holding something back.

Kheppy padded along the armchair's backrest.

"You left the bed," she said, her voice thick with sleep. "I was cold."

"I tried not to wake you," I said.

She sniffed and hopped down beside me, but she watched Lila and sniffed the air.

"You smell like you are thinking," the cat announced.

"It's that obvious?" Lila asked with a hint of a smile.

"Yes," Kheppy said, then turned in a circle and settled on my lap, a warm puff of fur.

The detective on the television solved his case with logical efficiency.

Lucky man.

Eventually, Lila's eyes closed. Her head tipped back against the couch, and a few minutes later her breathing deepened into sleep.

I stood quietly and pulled the blanket over her shoulders.

Kheppy jumped down and followed me into the kitchen while I rinsed our mugs.

"She is troubled," Kheppy said.

"I know."

Kheppy watched me for a moment, her tail swaying slowly.

"You cannot protect her from everything."

"I'm starting to realize that," I said.

Silence settled between us before she spoke again.

"The best way to help her is to find the truth," she said.

She was right, I couldn't deny it.

"I suppose that starts with a conversation with Howard," I said and glanced at the wall clock.

Dawn was only a few hours away. If Howard was hiding something, I would know soon enough.

One way or another.

Chapter 16

The Unthinkable

THE MORNING SUN GLIMMERED against the wet streets like someone had polished the town overnight. The storm had passed, leaving Laguna Bay washed clean and smelling faintly of eucalyptus and damp pavement. I breathed it in as I steered into town, Kheppy sitting on the passenger seat with her gaze glued to the window.

"You're driving more slowly than usual," she said, her ears twitching like she could sense my growing unease.

"I'm enjoying the sunshine," I said.

She gave me a look that said she didn't believe me.

Fine. I was stalling, and she knew it.

The truth was, I'd been feeling a little queasy since I woke up. Howard was a friend, and usually he was one of the people I turned to when things turned dicey. Steady as stone and kind to boot. But he'd been on edge at the party, and apparently he'd had words with Claire.

I didn't want to think it meant anything, but Evangeline's murder was making me second-guess everyone. Even people I cared about.

"I hate this," I muttered.

"Hate what?" Kheppy asked.

"Not trusting people." My fingers tightened on the wheel. "Howard wouldn't hurt a fly."

"But?" she pressed.

"But," I sighed, "I need to know what he, Neal, and Cornelia were arguing about. Maybe he thought he was protecting the community. Or maybe it has something to do with his argument with Claire. I don't know."

The sign for the Boo-tique appeared on the left. I drove past it.

Then I hit my turn signal and swung into the next driveway so sharply it tossed Kheppy against the car door.

"This is not the way to the hardware store," she said.

"I know. I'm stopping at the shop first."

Kheppy grimaced. "Oh? Something of grave importance suddenly came up?"

"Sissy's been working hard," I said.

"You are stalling," she said.

"Maybe a little," I admitted.

She narrowed her gaze. "You're only delaying the invincible."

"Inevitable," I grumbled. But I had to wonder if she was fumbling the phrase intentionally to make a point.

I parked along the curb and circled around to let her out.

"Okay. Maybe I'm stalling," I admitted as I opened the door and scooped her up. "But it is my business, and even if I have an exceptional clerk taking care of things, I shouldn't abandon it completely."

Kheppy didn't argue, which, frankly, I took as a small miracle.

A few puddles remained on the sidewalk from the storm, and a slight chill clung to the air. I shifted Kheppy against my chest with one arm and reached for the shop door key.

Then froze.

The shop's lights were already on.

"Huh," I murmured.

Entering, I spotted Sissy behind the counter, humming as she reorganized what looked like a brand-new arrangement of autumn-themed candles. She turned as the bell chimed.

"Good morning, Boo," she said brightly. "You're early. I thought you'd be spending time with Lila."

That's probably what I should have been doing. My brain scrambled for an excuse.

"I didn't want to overload you," I said. "You've been working so hard."

Sissy beamed. "I don't mind. Honestly, it's fun."

That was when I finally took in the room and felt a small pinch in my heart.

The place had been transformed. Petunia stood proudly in the window, garlands of red-gold leaves curled along the shelves, and the air smelled of cinnamon and caramel apple candles.

It all looked gloriously festive and autumnal—and I'd had nothing to do with it.

"Wow," I said, setting Kheppy on the counter so I could take in all of Sissy's work properly. "You've really outdone yourself."

She blushed. "Well, the holiday is coming up, so I'm hoping the new display gets some attention. I found this A-frame sign in the office and thought we could put it on the sidewalk to attract pedestrians. What do you think?"

She held it up to show me a charming chalk drawing of a turkey alongside the message: Gobble Up These Deals!

I vaguely remembered buying it over the summer and promptly forgetting about it.

I swallowed as I watched her. Young, eager, bright as sunshine. A small twinge of irrelevance passed through me, but it was quickly followed by something warmer. Pride. She'd stepped up in ways I never would have expected.

"Excellent work," Kheppy said suddenly.

Sissy jumped, her eyes widening as she turned back toward the talking cat now sitting primly on the counter.

"Sorry," she said, letting out a shaky laugh. "You can still surprise me, Kheppy. But thank you. Truly. A compliment from a remarkable creature such as yourself means more than you can imagine."

Kheppy's nose twitched with pleasure. "You're quite remarkable yourself."

Sissy beamed. Then her phone chimed.

The screen lit up as she pulled the device to her ear, but I caught the name before she turned away.

"This isn't a good time," Sissy said as she headed toward the office for privacy.

I looked at Kheppy to see if she'd seen the name on the phone's screen too.

"That was Darren Landon," I whispered, in case she hadn't. "I was wondering how those new werewolf family connections were going. Sounds like they might be a little strained."

"Apparently so," Kheppy said.

I drifted toward the front window and straightened a display of pumpkin-spice-scented hand soap while Sissy spoke in the back room. I couldn't make out the words, just the tension threaded through them.

My jaw tightened. Sissy had already suffered more upheaval than anyone her age deserved. Being wedged between two families—one human, one very much not—felt especially unfair.

She came back a moment later, trying to act casual.

It wasn't convincing.

"That was Darren," she said. "He invited me to have Thanksgiving dinner with his family."

"That's unexpectedly cordial," I said. Werewolves weren't exactly known for their social graces.

"That's what I thought," she said. "But there's no way I'm going without my mom and dad. And you know my dad. He has no idea about any of this supernatural stuff. Mom wants to keep it that way."

I nodded. Beth Meyers, who was born into a werepanther family but had never developed the ability to shift, had built a careful, human life after leaving her clan. Wyatt Landon had known exactly what he was doing when he arranged for her to adopt Sissy, his half-blood, biological daughter. Complicated didn't begin to cover it.

"That's a rough spot to be in," I said.

"It is what it is," Sissy replied, though the brightness in her voice had gone brittle. "And Darren isn't doing it out of the goodness of his heart. He's been trying to butter me up for days now."

I didn't know Darren Landon as well as I knew his father, but I knew enough to be concerned. "Why's that?"

She hesitated. Then:

"He wants me to talk to you on his behalf."

I frowned. "About what?"

"You might not know this, but the werewolves want a seat on the Midnight Council," she said carefully. "They want one of their own to join the elders."

I was vaguely aware of their efforts, but I still nearly dropped the ceramic pumpkin I was holding. "Why," I asked slowly, "would Darren think I have anything to do with making that happen?"

"They think you could help sway Howard's vote," she said.

I felt my stomach drop. "They want me to pressure a friend?"

The way she stared at her fidgeting fingers made it clear how uncomfortable the whole thing made her. "They know Cornelia's a hard no. All that bad blood between vampires and wolves. Neal said he'd support it, but

Howard's on the fence. The Landons think you might be able to sway him their way."

"Hold on," I said. "Say that even happens, they still need High Council approval. That's the big hurdle."

Sissy's expression turned sheepish. "Darren has already been working on that. He found out a regional liaison was blocking his requests until she could visit Laguna Bay."

She didn't have to say who the regional liaison was. The apology on her face said it all.

"What happened to your mother-in-law was awful," she said, "but as far as Darren is concerned, it means the High Council no longer has an excuse to delay his request. He's already contacted them about expediting the pack's petition."

I knew Sissy felt bad sharing that. She thought it made the Landons seem callous.

I saw it differently.

A possible motive for murder.

Sissy noticed my concern. "Gosh, Boo, I'm sorry. You have so much going on. You definitely don't need to hear about all this weird werewolf drama."

"It's not weird," I said. "You can always talk to me about anything."

But in the back of my mind, something chilled. Something clicked.

This "weird" drama might be the reason Evangeline ended up dead.

"Boo?" Sissy asked softly. "Are you okay?"

"Just thinking." It was the truth, even if it felt like the ground was shaking beneath me.

I glanced at the clock. Nearly nine. Howard would be at the hardware store by now—sweeping up sawdust, fussing with his shelves, or sorting through the endless varieties of nails and screws he insisted on keeping in stock.

"I should get going," I said, turning toward the counter to scoop up Kheppy.

"Don't worry about a thing," Sissy said. "I can handle everything here."

"I know you can." And she really could. The realization warmed me more than it stung.

Kheppy leaped neatly onto my shoulder, her tail settling against my collarbone like a fuzzy scarf. "Are you ready?" she asked softly.

"Probably not," I whispered back. "But I need answers."

Chapter 17

Mee-ow

As I pulled up to Howard's hardware shop, the sun was still struggling to break through the blanket of gray clouds, but the air smelled so fresh and clean I almost didn't mind the cold. For a moment, I lingered in my car just to breathe it in.

But not for long. I had a mission.

I scooped up Kheppy from the passenger seat and gave her a pointed look. "Remember. Not a word. Not even a whisper. There might be normies around."

She swished her tail and lifted her chin. "I probably know the risks even better than you do. I've certainly been around longer."

"I know," I muttered. "We just don't need to add mass panic over a talking cat to our troubles."

After an agonizingly long pause, she replied, "Mee-ow."

"Your restraint is appreciated," I said as I shut the car door and headed toward the store.

The place looked as charming as ever—faded slate-blue paint, striped awning, and big front windows displaying everything from beach umbrellas to galvanized watering cans. Somehow the little shop had survived Laguna Bay's hundred and fifty-year evolution without losing its soul.

The bell over the door jingled as I stepped inside. The familiar scent of cedar, rubber, and metal settled around me. A couple of customers browsed the beach-chair aisle, but otherwise the place felt quiet and peaceful.

Then I heard the shuffle of boxes from the back.

Found him.

Howard was crouched at the tarp shelf, stacking bright blue packages onto a shelf. His scant white hair was carefully combed over his freckled bald head. His flannel shirt-sleeves were rolled up, revealing forearms that had clearly spent a lifetime lifting sacks of potting soil and bundles of two-by-fours.

He turned at the sound of my footsteps. "Well now! New hair? Looks good."

I reached up, my fingertips brushing over the soft curls. "Thank you. Neal did it."

Howard chuckled. "Should've known. The guy knows his stuff. And hello to you too, Kheppy. Always good to see you."

"Meow," she replied, the sound edged with particular emphasis.

I scratched her head in silent solidarity. "Busy morning?" I asked.

"You know how it is," he said, sliding another tarp into place. "The rain comes, and suddenly everybody realizes they've got leaky roofs. How's the Boo-tique holding up? Is Merle's patch still doing the job?"

"So far, so good," I said. Though it occurred to me I should probably inspect it to be sure.

Howard stacked another couple of tarps, then wiped his hands on his jeans. "If you need one of these, or nails or sealant—anything—you let me know."

His kindness made me feel worse about why I was there.

Kheppy nudged her head under my chin, as if to remind me not to chicken out.

"Actually," I began, clearing my throat, "I was hoping we could talk."

He stiffened. "About what?"

"It might be better in private," I added quickly, glancing toward the door. The customers from earlier were walking out.

Howard's expression shifted. Concern first, then caution. "I'm pretty sure we're the only ones here."

"Better safe than sorry," I said.

He studied me for a moment, then nodded. "Come on."

He led me to his office, which was a generous use of the term. The tiny room held a battered desk, a couple of chairs, and tattered certificates and legal documents posted on the wall. The ocean-view window was its only saving grace.

Howard settled into the chair behind the desk and angled the security monitor toward himself so he could watch the front of the store. I sat in the guest chair, Kheppy perched politely on my lap like an elegant throw pillow.

"What's on your mind?" he asked.

After Sissy had dropped the werewolves' bombshell on me, the nosy neighbor cover story seemed like a waste of time. I got right to the point.

"You seemed out of sorts at the party." My palms suddenly felt clammy. I wiped them on my jeans and glanced at Kheppy for reassurance before looking back at him. "Willa mentioned seeing you, Cornelia, and Neal arguing, and I can't deny the timing bothers me."

His hand shot up, stopping me. "What are you trying to say, Boo?"

I folded my hands together to stop them from trembling. "If you did something drastic, even something you thought would help, please tell me." I held his gaze. "The police will piece it together eventually. If it was an accident or a mistake, we need to get ahead of it and make sure it doesn't backfire on the community."

Howard's eyebrows shot up. He leaned back in his chair, one hand going to his forehead, as if he needed a second to catch up with where this conversation had gone.

"No," he said, the word coming out hard and sharp. Then he shook his head. "If you're asking if I hurt Evangeline, the answer is no. Not on purpose, not by accident. Not at all."

As I watched him, I realized I wasn't looking at guilt. It was frustration. Maybe even fear, but not the kind that comes from having done something unforgivable and getting caught. I'd walked in here prepared for the worst. This wasn't it.

"You're right," he continued. "I was annoyed and irritated, even angry, but..."

He paused, and I could see he wanted to say more. Something was holding him back.

I couldn't let him shut me out. Not now.

"Was it about the werewolves? I know they want their elder seat back."

His eyes widened. "How do you know about that?"

"Darren told Sissy," I said.

He sighed and seemed to relax. "Then you know Neal and Cornelia were forcing me to be the deciding vote. Cowards. So, if you think about it, I was the last person who wanted to see Evangeline dead. Whether she ultimately lobbied the High Council to revoke our sanctuary charter or not, as long as she was alive, she was going to make sure that petition never came up for a vote. She wasn't the forgiving type, as you of all people well know."

Boy, was that the truth. But that wasn't the most startling part of what he'd said.

"Are you sure she was that dead set against their request?" I asked.

"She said as much in her report to the High Council. She shared it with Cornelia, Neal, and me a few days before she arrived," he said. He sighed and leaned back. "I don't get it. The Landon pack had an elder seat, and they abandoned it."

"That was thirty years ago," I said. "A lot has changed since then."

"Maybe it has." He tapped his fingers on the desk. "But if they want to be part of this community again, there's nothing stopping them from doing it." He met my gaze directly. "Why not get more involved and show some good faith? Why the urgency?"

He'd just voiced the same question that had been nagging at me.

"I don't know," I said. "But now that Evangeline is gone, I think they're eager to take advantage of this window of opportunity."

A shadow passed over him. Sadness? Distrust? It was hard to tell.

I swallowed hard. "Do you think the werewolves could have had something to do with her death?"

His expression shifted, but it wasn't surprise, which told me he'd already considered the possibility.

"No," he said. "I can't believe they would resort to murder just to get a council seat. I don't even know how they'd pull it off."

I wanted to agree. I wanted the kind of certainty Howard seemed to have. But the sick feeling in my gut refused to budge. I couldn't rule it out. Not yet.

My list of viable suspects was dwindling fast, but there was someone who still stood out.

"Do you know anyone who might have had a grudge against Evangeline?" I asked. "Someone with a particular reason to be angry with her?"

I hoped he'd take the bait.

He didn't.

He shook his head and kept his mouth shut.

If he were being completely honest with me, there was someone he would have mentioned.

Kheppy knew exactly what I was doing, and I felt her small chest rise and fall with a sorrowful sigh.

"I ask because a few people saw you arguing with Claire at the party," I said.

His jaw muscle twitched.

"Oh," he said in a tense, measured voice. "That. Claire... well... she can fixate on things, especially when they involve animals."

I frowned. "Or their ghosts?"

He scanned the ceiling like the answers he was searching for were written there.

They weren't.

"Or injustice or cruelty or dark magic?" I added.

"Look," he said at last, "Claire has a good heart, but sometimes she goes too far. You'd think she'd learn from her mistakes."

My pulse stuttered. "Mistakes?"

He shook his head. "I shouldn't have said anything."

Oh, no. He wasn't going to shut me out now.

"Do you think Claire might have hurt Evangeline because Evangeline hurt her cat?" I said in a rush.

He glared at me, then shook his head. "I really couldn't say."

"Is that because you don't know or because you're protecting her?"

"That's probably a question for Claire, don't you think?"

Before I could try again, I realized the time, and winced. "I was supposed to meet Merle for lunch."

I fired off a quick apology text to him. He replied instantly.

No rush, come whenever you're done.

Always so forgiving.

I turned my attention back to Howard. "I should let you get back to work."

Howard rose when I did. "Boo?"

"Yes?" I scooped up Kheppy in the crook of my arm and turned to the door.

He scratched the top of his head. "Mind if I offer some unsolicited advice?"

I braced. "Is it about minding my own business?"

"No." His smile was warm but weary. "It's about Merle."

I hugged Kheppy a little closer. "What about him?"

"Whatever is happening between the two of you, he's in. All the way in. But he'll also step back the instant he thinks you want space. Not because that's what he wants, but because he might think that's what you want."

My breath caught. "Did he say something to you?"

Howard didn't answer that. Instead, he said, "If that's not what you want, you might want to tell him before he starts misreading the signs."

I hated how much truth there was in that unsolicited advice.

As we stepped out of the office and back into the shop, the bell chimed overhead, and a fresh breeze drifted in with a customer whose anxious gaze scanned the length of one aisle and then the next before Howard asked if the young man needed help.

"Do you carry tarps?" the customer asked. "My roof has a leak."

As Howard led him to the display, I walked with Kheppy cradled against my chest.

I stepped onto the sidewalk, the meager sunshine warming my face, but all I felt was the cold creep of dread.

Kheppy murmured in my ear as I opened the car's passenger door. "You are worried."

I set her down on the cushion and swallowed hard. "Of course I'm worried. I came here for answers, but I ended up with more questions. And now a Merle-sized problem on top of everything else."

Kheppy nudged my palm. "At least," she said, "you are not facing it alone."

No, I wasn't.

At least there was that.

Chapter 18

Out to Lunch

When I pulled out of the hardware store's parking lot, the midday sun had dried most of the puddles. Only the scent of wet asphalt lingered.

I glanced at Kheppy, sprawled across the passenger seat. "Are you sure you want to wait in the car? I can drop you off at the Boo-tique first."

She stretched, her white front paws catching a ray of sunshine. "I'm sure. It's comfortable in here." Her gaze narrowed. "Are you putting off facing Merle?"

I nearly drove into a fire hydrant.

"No," I said, indignant—or trying to be. My voice wobbled, which ruined the whole effect.

Kheppy's tail twitched. "Mm-hmm. I don't believe you."

I huffed. "Howard just caught me off guard with his warning about Merle. He made it sound like I've been sending signals. Or something."

"You *have* been sending something," she said dryly.

"Thanks," I muttered. "That's not helpful."

We reached Beachside Café, and I slid into an open parking spot on the street. Almost instantly, savory smells from the kitchen mingled with the salty breeze rolling in from the shore. For a long moment, I sat behind the wheel, listening to the click of the cooling engine. I didn't want to admit it, but Kheppy had been right about one thing.

"I hope Merle doesn't think I've been pulling away," I said. "It's been a difficult time. That's all. I've had a lot going on."

Kheppy glanced up at me and cocked her head to the side. "It isn't that."

My breath hitched. "How do you know?"

"You are overthinking again," she said. "Cleopatra could juggle her affairs of state and her affairs of the heart without twisting herself into knots. If she could manage all that, surely you can handle a lunch date."

I let out a snort. "Sometimes I forget about your illustrious past. It's so kind of you to remind me." She occasionally struggled with sarcasm, so I laid it on extra thick before adding, "But you must know by now, I'm no Cleopatra."

"No," she allowed. "But you share certain qualities. Stubbornness, for instance."

"Oh, good. I'm royally stubborn. Good to know."

This wasn't a topic I wanted to pursue, so I focused on the café and spotted Merle almost immediately. He sat at a window table, hands wrapped around a tall glass like it might try to make a getaway. When his gaze met mine, his expression softened.

"He sees me," I murmured. "I'd better get in there."

Before climbing out, I reached over and cracked the passenger window to be sure Kheppy had fresh air. It wasn't wide enough for her to squeeze through, but I doubted that would stop her if she tried. "You promise you're not going anywhere?"

"Yes," she said primly. "I will, as you say, stay put. And you needn't worry, I won't go looking for Evangeline's killer without you."

"Good." I grabbed my purse from the backseat. "I'd rather not have to explain that to the detective."

I shut the door and headed for the café.

Inside, the place was warm and filled with the delicious scent of grilled burgers and fries. The murmur of lunch-goers mixed with the clatter of dishes. I spotted Merle standing as I approached, but something was different.

He didn't lean in for a hug.

Instead, he hovered—sweet, but nervous. Howard's words rang through me: *He'll step back the instant he thinks you want space.*

A pang of guilt hit me square in the chest.

"Hi," I said, settling into the seat opposite him.

"Hi," he echoed, smiling. "Glad you made it."

"I'm sorry I'm late. Things just ran long." I focused on smoothing the napkin onto my lap.

He nodded, as if that was a good excuse.

We both knew it wasn't.

I was about to launch into a better apology when something else caught my attention. It took me a few seconds to realize what felt off.

"Where's Chef Glen?" I asked, looking around.

Merle sighed. "The server said he's at city hall, checking out his new office."

It made sense, but it still seemed odd. "I guess I haven't gotten used to the fact that he's going to be our mayor." I paused. "If I haven't mentioned it lately, you've been an excellent sport about the whole thing."

Merle guffawed and sipped his soda as the server brought me a glass of ice water.

"I'm glad he won," he said. "We could do a lot worse than Glen Phan in the mayor's office." He leaned forward and lowered his voice. "I was only worried about representation for our community, anyway."

I lifted my water. "Cheers to that," I said, clinking his glass.

"Cheers."

He sipped, set down his glass, and studied me. "So, what's been keeping you so busy?"

"Well," I said faintly. "That's a loaded question."

I caught him up on what I'd learned using a mix of euphemisms, hand gestures, and mouthed words. I was reasonably sure anyone eavesdropping would think we were either talking about home repairs or unpleasant digestive issues.

After the server came to take our order and slipped away again, he leaned back slowly and filled me in on what he knew about Darren Landon and the pack's push for a Midnight Council seat, which was enough to confirm what I'd already heard from Sissy and Howard.

I matched him in kind—sharing enough to keep him in the loop, but not enough to drag him into the deeper worries I was still sorting out for myself.

"Has Howard mentioned anything about Claire Greenwood lately?" I asked.

"The woman who runs the pet cemetery?"

I nodded.

"Not much," he said. "I know he's met with her a few times, but he didn't elaborate. Why?"

I twisted the straw wrapper between my fingers. "Apparently, they were arguing at the party. Before, *you know*."

The shadow of Evangeline's death passed briefly between us.

"That doesn't sound like Howard," Merle said.

"That's what I thought," I said. "Any idea what could upset him like that?"

Merle rubbed his chin. "No. But maybe I'll swing by and talk to Claire. I'm scheduled to do a vacation check on a condominium near her place this afternoon."

"Are you sure that's a good idea?" I asked. I still wasn't sure I trusted that woman, but I trusted Merle.

"I'm not going to interrogate her," he said. "I'll just stop by and see what's up. No harm in that, right?"

I could tell by the look on his face that he wanted to help. Maybe he needed it as much as I did. We were so similar that way. "Isn't police business keeping you busy enough?"

He shrugged modestly. "I suppose so, but I'm never too busy to help you or the community. It's kind of what I do."

The server arrived with two steaming plates. My burger was huge and smelled exactly like the kind of meal Delphine would lecture me about, now that she'd gone vegan. But as far as I was concerned, it was mouthwatering bliss on a bun.

We drifted into lighter talk—Lila, Delphine, the usual things—and somewhere along the way, the heaviness in my chest eased.

For the first time all day, the murder wasn't the loudest thing in my head, and I let myself keep it that way.

After the last of our fries disappeared and the server whisked away our plates, Merle reached for the check.

"I've got it," he said.

"Merle—"

"No arguments. Please." His smile turned shy. "Let me do this."

I didn't know why that simple insistence made my heart swell, but it did.

When we stepped outside, the sun was bright enough to make the sidewalk almost glow. A gull screeched overhead.

Merle walked me to my car, his hands shoved awkwardly in his pockets.

"Let me know if you find out anything from Claire," I said.

"Will do." He cleared his throat. "Anything for you."

Maybe it was the sunlight. Maybe it was Howard's warning. Maybe it was how fragile everything felt, and how holding onto good things seemed more important than ever. But I rose onto my toes, took Merle's face in my hands, and kissed him.

A real kiss, not a peck or a brush across the cheek. A long, warm, deliberate kiss that left him slightly breathless when I pulled away.

He stared at me like I'd knocked something loose.

"Boo," he murmured. "Wow."

I smiled, feeling lighter than I had in a long time. "I'm lucky to have you in my life, Merle Foster," I said. "You know that, don't you?"

He nodded, slow and stunned and sweet. "Now I do."

I squeezed his arm and slipped into the driver's seat. My heart was still racing when I closed the door, and he strode away.

Kheppy's sleepy eyes blinked open from her nap in the passenger seat. "How was lunch?"

"Quite nice," I said as I started the engine. "Quite nice, indeed."

She stretched and hummed her approval. "I suppose Cleopatra's advice is still relevant."

"Oh no," I muttered, pulling out of the lot. "Please don't tell me you're going to quote that woman all afternoon."

She purred. "Only if you continue to need it."

I rolled my eyes, but didn't bother arguing. Not today.

Not when the air was clean, the sun was bright, and—for just a little while—I was letting myself feel like something in my life was finally going right.

Chapter 19
Good Vibes

YOU WOULDN'T THINK A single meal could change the whole tone of a day, but as I eased away from Beachside Café, something inside me shifted, like a lock finally giving way. Lunch with Merle had gone unexpectedly well. No awkward silences, no emotional landmines, just warm smiles and easy conversation. He'd listened. I'd listened. And unlike most of our recent interactions, we weren't tiptoeing around each other like nervous kids afraid to make eye contact.

It was nice.

For a few moments, I'd almost forgotten Evangeline's killer was still out there somewhere, and that our whole supernatural community might be in the police crosshairs because of it.

Almost.

Driving toward the Boo-tique, that familiar frustration crept back in. We were days into this mess, and I still had no idea who the killer was. I didn't even have a clear motive—just too many suspicions chasing each other in circles in my head.

The two I couldn't shake were the werewolves' sudden push to join the Midnight Council and Claire's odd behavior at the party. It bothered me even more knowing it had caught Howard's attention—and his ire.

Kheppy sat upright in the passenger seat, watching me. "You're obsessing again," she said, as if it were a bad habit I should've broken by now.

"No, I'm thinking," I said, my eyes locked on the road.

"In circles," she replied.

I glanced at her, waiting for another smart aleck response.

Instead, she leaned closer and brushed her cheek against my arm.

"You'll figure this out," she said at last. "You always do. Even when you don't believe you will. Give it time."

Sometimes she was infuriating. Other times—like now—she was the sweetest thing in my life.

"Thanks, Khep," I said. "I just don't know how much time we have."

When we reached the Boo-tique, the cheerful turkey sign was out on the sidewalk, inviting passersby to wander in and browse. I spotted Sissy tending to a rack of autumn-colored wreaths, her ponytail swinging behind her like a metronome. She'd been so dependable lately, taking over without a complaint, and I'd been grateful for it.

The bell chimed when I crossed the threshold and breathed in the familiar scent of lemon, eucalyptus, and sage from the shop's protection candle, burning away on its usual shelf.

"The wreaths look terrific," I said.

Sissy spun around. "Boo! How was lunch?"

"Good." I smiled at the memory. "Really good." I glanced around. Had she dusted the shelves too? I dragged a finger across one. Spotless. "Have you been cleaning?"

Her cheeks reddened. "A little. I had some extra time."

"Have I told you what a great job you're doing?" I set Kheppy on the counter, where she immediately strutted over to her favorite spot beside the window. "I hope you took a lunch break."

Sissy made a sheepish face. "Not yet. I brought left-overs, but I wanted to finish this first."

"You deserve something better than leftovers." I pulled out my wallet and fanned a few bills. "Lunch is on me. Go treat yourself."

Her eyes widened. "That's really sweet, but you don't have to."

"I want to." I pressed the money into her hand. "Go. Enjoy something special. Doctor's orders. Or Boo's orders."

Her smile was small but genuine. "All right. If you insist. I heard your friend's gelato shop has a new caramel apple flavor. Doesn't that sound delicious?"

I snorted. "Only in Southern California would someone crave what's basically fancy ice cream after a cold, rainy day."

"The sun is out now," Kheppy observed, peering through the window.

Sissy giggled. "See? She gets it." Sissy grabbed her jacket and headed for the door. "I'll be back soon!"

"Take your time," I called after her.

The bell jingled as she left.

The shop settled into a hush, broken by the hum of the mini fridge and a slow, melancholy pop song drifting from the speakers.

"Oh no," I said as I caught the tune. "We're not listening to Sissy's mopey playlist today."

I walked over to the silver cube tucked behind the register and switched it from her preset list to the radio station that played the hits from my generation.

A happy, folksy Celtic fiddle riff burst through the sound system, followed by a guy calling for someone named Eileen.

Kheppy sat up and, in the DJ's smooth baritone, announced, "You're listening to KQZE Laguna Bay, where the eighties rock and the good vibes roll."

I burst out laughing. "You sound better than Southland Sam himself. If you're not careful, they might put you on the air."

"That would not be wise, Boo," she said primly in her own voice.

I rubbed her head, grabbed the clipboard with Sissy's inventory checklist, and stepped behind the counter. Inventory was usually the bane of a shopkeeper's existence, but I found it strangely soothing. Everything tallied, tidy, and accounted for.

If only murder investigations were that simple.

As I marked down the number of plastic cauldrons left in stock, I felt the tension at the back of my neck loosen. The familiar clutter—cinnamon-scented brooms, feathered masks, plushy black cats—had always comforted me.

Even so, today the calm felt fragile.

Kheppy hopped onto the counter beside me. "You are humming."

I froze. "I am not."

"And smiling. Humans only do that when they are—"

"Don't say another word," I said, cutting her off. "Don't jinx it."

"Understood," she said, and we left it at that.

I worked while she napped, and an hour slipped by before the bell chimed again.

Sissy walked in carrying a Beachside Café paper bag and munching on a fry.

I raised a brow. "Changed your mind about the gelato?"

She shook her head. "The place was closed. So I got garlic fries instead."

"That's strange. Jemma doesn't usually close for lunch." I looked at my watch. It was well past that. That didn't sit right. I grabbed my phone from the office to call her and see what was up. Before I could, the shop phone rang.

Sissy wiped her hands on a napkin and picked up. "Halloween Boo-tique, this is Sissy... Hi, Merle, she's right here." She handed me the receiver.

I took it. "Hello?"

"Boo?" Merle's voice was strained. "Why didn't you answer your phone? I've been trying to reach you."

"What happened?" My heart jumped as I noticed the notifications stacked on my screen.

Three missed calls. Five texts.

All from Merle.

A cold wave slid down my back.

"Sorry. I've been working on inventory and didn't have it with me. What's going on? Are you okay?"

A beat of silence followed, long enough for me to imagine at least a half-dozen grim scenarios.

"I'm fine," he said, "but Claire isn't. When I went by her place, the police were there."

I gripped the edge of the desk. "Why?"

"An officer was putting her in the back of a cruiser. She's in custody."

I nearly dropped the phone.

Jemma would have to wait. Finding out what was happening with Claire had just become my number one priority.

Chapter 20

Plant Tonic

Claire was in custody.

Merle's words were still rattling inside my head after I slid my phone into my pocket and found myself standing in the Boo-tique near the baked-apple-scented candles and a drooping pothos. For a moment, I honestly couldn't remember what I'd been doing before he called.

Was this what Detective Platt was alluding to when he said evidence was pointing the investigation in another direction?

The wall clock read a little past two-thirty. Outside, the earlier clouds had burned off, and a weak strip of sunlight cut across the floor, but it did nothing for the fog in my head.

I couldn't ignore the pattern anymore. Every time I stopped thinking of Claire as a viable suspect, something pushed her back to the top of the list.

And this was the most dramatic push yet.

For Willa's sake, I'd wanted her to be innocent. I'd convinced myself my instincts were off base. But it was looking like my instincts had been right all along.

"Why are you staring at that plant?" Kheppy asked from her perch by the aromatherapy oils.

I shook myself out of the trance and reached for the water bottle tucked beneath the cash register. The one Delphine kept filled with her special plant tonic, which was, as far as I could tell, just rice water with a dose of her aggressively optimistic grow charm. I also grabbed one of my favorite orange sodas from the mini fridge.

"I'm working," I said, mostly to convince myself. "The pothos looks thirsty. If Delphine notices I haven't been watering it properly, she'll have a conniption."

Kheppy hopped down and trailed after me as I worked my way toward the hanging plant by the front window. A few of its leaves were wilting enough to make me worry.

As the tonic glugged out of the bottle, I tried to make sense of Claire's situation. That's when Sissy swept in, fresh from collecting the day's mail. The envelopes rustled in her hand as she slowed, her sneakers squeaking on the floor. She stopped dead, stared at me, then at the bottle in my hand.

"Boo?" Her voice had that careful, customer-service lilt she used on touchy people. "Are you all right?"

"Of course," I said. "Why wouldn't I be?"

She pointed at my hand. "You're watering the plant with orange soda."

I froze, mid-pour. A fat orange droplet slid off a pothos leaf and onto the floor with a small, sticky splash.

I looked at the bottle in my hand. Bright label. Even brighter liquid. In my other hand was Delphine's homemade plant tonic.

"For crying out loud," I muttered.

Kheppy padded away in the opposite direction, her amusement contained for my sake, but just barely.

Sissy hugged the mail to her chest, her eyes wide, as she dashed to the back. "I'll grab the paper towels."

I snorted, the sound coming out more tired than frustrated. "No, doll. I've got it. I just hope this poor thing recovers. All those chemicals and carbonation can't be good for it."

"It probably won't kill it," Sissy called back.

She didn't sound convincing.

"Claire's in police custody, and I'm watering plants with soda," I said under my breath.

By the time I reached the counter, Sissy already had a roll of paper towels waiting for me. I thanked her and took it back to the mess.

Her expression softened as she followed me. "You've got a lot on your mind. I heard you on the phone before. Was that Merle?"

"Yeah," I said. "He said the police were taking Claire to the station."

Guilt washed over me, both for suspecting Claire and for not suspecting her enough. It was a familiar tug-of-war, never being sure if I was being too hard on people or not hard enough.

"I thought..." Sissy began, then stopped. "I mean, she always seemed so nice. Kept to herself mostly, but—"

"I know." I wiped off my sticky fingers and set the orange soda back on the counter. "I was hoping we were all wrong, but it seems she had some trouble before she came to Laguna Bay."

Sissy chewed her bottom lip, then straightened with a kind of resolve. "You should probably go home," she said. "Let your sister and Lila know what happened. I can take care of things here."

"I can just call them," I protested, because it was the reasonable thing to do. Also, because leaving my shop in the middle of the day still felt like deserting a post.

She gave me a look that said I was underestimating both her and the Boo-tique. "If it gets busy, I'll text you. I'm sure it'll be a relief to Lila to know the focus of the case has shifted."

Behind me, Kheppy hopped lightly onto a display shelf. "You know she's right," she said.

I sighed, defeated. "Fine. Just let me finish cleaning up this mess so we don't get ants."

"You don't have to do that," Sissy said. "I was going to mop this afternoon anyway."

I relented, scooped up Kheppy, and grabbed my purse from the shelf beneath the register. The little bell over the door chimed as we stepped outside.

For all my grumbling, there was relief in the idea of going home. Of telling Lila in person that the police had someone else in their sights. Of course the case wasn't solved yet. But for the first time in days, the suspect in the crosshairs wasn't my daughter.

That had to count for something. It had to.

But as I headed for the car, one thought refused to settle—

If Claire was in custody, why didn't this feel like it was over?

Chapter 21

Home Again

THE DRIVE HOME FROM the Boo-tique was trickier than usual as I steered around the palm fronds and torn tree branches scattered by the earlier rainstorm. Laguna Bay got so little rain and wind that even a modest storm made it look like it had survived a small catastrophe.

Kheppy sat in the passenger seat, watching me. "You're exceptionally quiet," she observed.

"I'm thinking about Claire," I said.

"I figured as much."

"If she did it—if she hurt Evangeline—I can't help wondering if it had something to do with Saphira and seeking justice for that sweet creature," I said. "If I'd known, maybe I could have done something."

There it was again—that familiar, stubborn wish to save people from themselves.

It surfaced more often than I liked to admit.

"You aren't responsible for the choices other people make," Kheppy said.

"Don't let Delphine hear you say that. She'll put it on a motivational mug and hand it to me for my next birthday."

Kheppy stretched and settled into a comfortable spot. "But it's true."

Unfortunately, she probably had a point.

By the time we turned onto our little dirt lane, the sun was casting long shadows across the front yard. I slowed when I spotted familiar cars scattered along the fence line. My garden-witch friends were here.

The knot in my chest eased a notch. As Kheppy and I approached the front door, voices drifted from inside, bright and cheerful. My heart lifted.

I threw open the door and looked for Lila, but only the others were gathered around the kitchen table, sifting through recipe cards and cookbooks.

"Am I interrupting something?" I asked, setting my keys on the cabinet by the door.

Delphine glanced up, her gray braids coiled around her head like a crown, a pencil tucked behind her ear. "We're just going over the Thanksgiving menu," she said.

Willa nudged her reading glasses higher on her nose. "There's so much to do, and only a couple of days left," she added, worry etched into the fine lines at the corners of her eyes.

She wasn't wrong. But given we were in the middle of a murder investigation, it hardly felt like the most pressing concern.

Beside her, Opal and Jemma were flipping through handwritten note cards.

"I'm surprised you're not at the gelato shop," I said to Jemma, keeping my tone light. "Kids are out of school, and the sun's out."

She shrugged. "I can afford to take an afternoon off."

I knew all that gung-ho entrepreneurial spirit would wear her down eventually.

Delphine's gaze sharpened. "Why are *you* home in the middle of the business day, Boo? Did something happen?"

"It did, actually." I looked around for my daughter. "Where's Lila? I have news for her."

"She went for a walk about an hour ago," my sister said. "Wanted to stretch her legs on the trail. Can't say I blame her. She slept pretty late. What's the news?"

I sank into a chair. "Merle saw the police taking Claire into custody. He didn't know if it was in connection with Evangeline's case, but it would seem pretty likely."

Opal's hand flew to her mouth. Willa froze. Jemma gasped and shook her head.

"I know I've had my suspicions about her," I said, "but we shouldn't jump to any conclusions. We don't have all the facts yet."

My gaze landed on Willa. She shifted in her chair, eyes fixed on anything but me.

"Unless you know something," I said, my tone heavy with suspicion.

"Of course not," she said. "Do you think I'd keep something like that from you?"

Silence settled over the room, punctuated by the soft rumble of the kettle coming to a boil on the stove.

Delphine jumped to pull it off the heat. As she did, she frowned at my shirt.

"What on earth happened to you?"

I looked down at the orange stain spreading across my I'm-Not-Everyone's-Cup-of-Tea T-shirt.

"Shop accident," I said.

"An unfortunate incident with the plant tonic," Kheppy added.

"Very minor," I said and scooped her up before she could elaborate. "I should probably change."

I hauled Kheppy down the hall to my bedroom. Once the door was shut behind us, I glared at her.

"You didn't have to elaborate," I scolded.

"But you did try to fertilize the plants with orange soda," Kheppy said as she licked her paw and dragged it over her ear.

I wanted to argue, but it was never wise to argue with Kheppy when she was right. So I focused on finding a clean shirt.

"Do you think I was too hard on Willa?" I asked when I was nearly ready to rejoin the others. I couldn't shake the fact that my friend wouldn't meet my eyes.

Kheppy tilted her head. "Why? Do you think she knows something about Claire she isn't telling you?"

"She definitely knows more than she's letting on," I said. "I just don't understand why she's holding back. We're friends. At least I thought we were."

When we returned to the kitchen, Delphine and Opal were at the counter, assembling a tea tray. Steam curled from the pot's spout. A plate of cookies sat beside it, sugar crystals glinting faintly in the overhead light.

Willa and Jemma had moved to the sofa, where they sat with their heads bent together, their voices hushed and urgent.

As I entered the room, I caught my name, then Claire's.

"...should have told her sooner," Willa was saying.

"She knows now," Jemma replied. "Just watch, it'll all work out. Trust me. The police know what they're doing. It's a relief, if you think about it."

There was a note in her tone I hadn't heard before. Not relief exactly. More like confidence.

Even though Claire's misfortune meant Lila was probably off the hook, that cavalier attitude felt all kinds of wrong.

When I settled into the armchair beside them, they spun toward me, surprised. "If you two are breathing easier just because Claire's in custody, I should remind you that we still don't know if she's guilty. And the longer this investigation goes, the worse it is for all of us. It's putting the whole supernatural community at risk."

"Boo," Willa said, cheeks flushing. "We were just—"

"Talking about Claire," I finished. "I know. I heard."

Jemma tried to backpedal. "But it is good news for Lila. If the police think they've found Evangeline's killer, that takes suspicion off her, right?"

"I suppose so," I said. "But there's more to Claire's story. Isn't there?"

My gaze landed on Willa. "Why weren't you honest about her? You never mentioned knowing her family, or that she had trouble in her hometown."

Her eyes shimmered. For a second, I thought she might burst into tears. Instead, she drew herself up, fingers worrying the hem of her sweater like she might rub a hole through it.

"How do you know about that?" she demanded.

"Howard told me."

Instantly, the fight drained out of her. "Oh."

"Why didn't you tell me?" I pressed.

Some of her defiance returned. "I told you already. That is her story to tell."

"Except she hasn't," I said. "And now the police are involved. Did you allow us to welcome a killer into our community?"

"Claire is not a killer," Willa protested.

It was exactly what I'd expect from Willa.

"Howard doesn't know what she went through," she added. "Claire went through a rough patch, but it wasn't her fault, and she's worked hard to put that past behind her."

I could understand the desire to protect someone with a painful past, but this was bigger than one person's privacy. This put the safety of our community at risk.

"Are you saying there's no chance she'll be arrested for Evangeline's murder?" I asked.

Willa flinched. Guilt flashed across her face.

I'd say that was a no.

Jemma squeezed Willa's hand. "Boo, please," she said. "We're all shaken. The important thing is that the police have her. They'll get to the truth. That's their job, right? And we can get back to normal."

Normal. I wasn't sure I even knew what that meant anymore.

Across the room, Delphine and Opal arrived with the tea tray, the porcelain rattling as my sister set it on the coffee table.

"Can I interest anyone in a fresh cup or the last of the lemon bars?" she asked brightly, trying to cut the tension.

Opal gave me a meaningful look over her glasses. "We're all on the same side here. We want the truth, and we want to keep everyone safe. Let's not lose sight of that."

I wanted to believe her. I really did.

But something in the room didn't feel right.

Like we were all having the same conversation, but hearing an entirely different message.

"Fine," I said. "Tea now. Questions later."

I took the cup Delphine handed me. It was a rich, earthy blend with a touch of sweet vanilla that should have soothed me. It didn't.

This afternoon, the walls of the house felt too close, the energy in the room too thick with worry.

And no one else seemed bothered by it.

If I stayed here, I was either going to snap at someone I loved or eat my way through the treat plate.

"I need some fresh air," I said suddenly, jumping up and grabbing my jacket from the peg by the door. "I'm going for a walk. Maybe I can find Lila and tell her about Claire."

Delphine frowned. "Do you want company?"

"No." I softened it with a small smile. "I'll be fine. Besides, somebody needs to plan Thanksgiving. If you leave it to me, we might end up with drive-through burgers again."

"Oh, that was an interesting year," Opal said, shaking her head at the memory of that unfortunate time they'd all caught the flu, and I'd tried to pull together the feast by myself. It had not gone well.

Kheppy hopped down from the armchair and padded to my side, her tail brushing against my ankle. "I will join you," she said.

I was about to tell her I wouldn't be good company, but I had a feeling she already knew that. So, I slipped on the jacket and headed for the back door with her close behind.

I told myself I just needed to find Lila and maybe a little time to think.

But deep down, I knew better.

I wasn't trying to clear my head.

I was trying to figure out what everyone else seemed willing to ignore.

And how to fix something that might already be beyond repair.

Chapter 22
Overlook

THE BACK DOOR STUCK a little, as usual, before it gave way with a low creak. As I stepped onto the porch, cold air enveloped me. I pulled my jacket tighter and squinted at the yard.

The grass and garden were still damp from the earlier storm. Patches of mud pocked the ground, and the trail behind the house was a darker ribbon cutting into the brush.

I looked down at my suede-and-sheepskin boots and sighed. I considered swapping them for a pair of old sneakers, but I'd wasted enough time already.

Kheppy brushed past my leg. "What's wrong? Too chilly for you?"

She loved to tease me about my thin skin, though if you asked me, she took that fur coat of hers for granted.

"I'm fine," I said, pressing onward. "Just waiting on you."

She gave me the feline equivalent of an eye roll and picked her way across the mostly dry yard. I followed, choosing each step with care.

The trail started at the back fence, where an old wooden gate leaned permanently open. I stepped through and onto the narrow path. As far as I was concerned, I had one job: find my daughter.

As Kheppy and I moved in silence, my mind kept circling Claire and Willa—my thoughts darting between frustration and anger.

When we reached the small overlook where an old fallen tree trunk lay on its side, Lila was sitting there, her long hair pulled into a low, loose knot, dark curls escaping and frizzing in the damp air. Beyond her, the valley unfurled in muted greens and browns, dotted here and there with rooftops and tree canopies.

My breath caught. For all the tension between us lately, she looked impossibly young in that moment. Not a middle-aged woman with an adult daughter and a complicated life of her own, but the little girl who used to stomp up this very hill, full of sass and vinegar.

"Should we join her?" Kheppy murmured.

"We should ask first," I whispered back.

Lila must have heard us, because she turned slightly.

"Hey, sweet pea," I called gently. "Mind if we sit?"

She hesitated, then scooted a few inches along the log. "Go ahead." Her voice was small and tired.

I stepped forward, careful to avoid the worst of the mud. Despite my best efforts, my boots had still picked up a few splatters.

I brushed at the bark and sat down. The wood was cold through the seat of my jeans. Kheppy leaped up and settled between us.

She stiffened at the sound of a barking dog in the distance, but relaxed once it stopped.

"I have news," I said. "The police picked up Claire Greenwood this afternoon. Merle told me it's probably in connection with your grandmother's case."

Lila's fingers tightened around a travel mug in her lap. "Yeah?" she asked. "She's a suspect?"

I half-nodded. "It's looking that way."

For one impossibly long moment, I waited for the reaction I'd been anticipating the whole walk up here. Relief loosening her shoulders. A sigh. Maybe one of those smiles I'd been hoarding in my memory.

Instead, a tear slid down her cheek.

My heart lurched. "Oh, honey. It probably means you're not a suspect anymore."

More tears followed. Lila swiped at them with the heel of her palm.

"I'm sorry," she whispered. "I'm so sorry."

"It's okay. You have nothing to be sorry about," I said, suddenly bewildered.

Kheppy edged closer, molding herself against my daughter's thigh. "Lila?" she said. "Your eyes are leaking."

Lila let out a choking, broken laugh. "It's called crying, but thank you."

"It was a joke," Kheppy said patiently. "I thought it would make you feel better."

"Oh, Khep." I pulled my furry friend into an embrace, too charmed to be frustrated at her poor comic timing. "You're such a sweetheart."

She nuzzled one hand while I rummaged through my pockets with the other, searching for a tissue or anything to offer Lila. I came up empty.

Lila pulled herself together without my help, just as she'd done for most of her life.

She set the travel mug on the ground, her fingers fumbling. Her breathing came in short, uneven bursts.

A terrible feeling settled over me. Why wasn't she relieved?

I planted both hands at my sides, bracing myself for the answer.

It took every ounce of willpower to force out the question I knew I had to ask: "Lila, what is it?"

When she didn't respond, I added, "Is there something you want to tell me?"

When she turned to me, my sweet girl's eyes were rimmed with fresh tears. Her nod almost undid me.

"I need to tell you something about Grandmama," she said. "About what the detective heard me say to Delphine, and why I couldn't say anything at the station. I thought if I stayed silent, maybe it would all go away."

"You don't have to tell me anything." Even as I said it, fear gripped me.

"I do," she said. "If it comes out, I want you to hear it from me first. I want you to know I didn't mean it. Not really."

Her words weren't making sense. Right then, nothing was.

"I said things a long time ago when I was angry. But that's all it was: anger," she said. "I didn't know she was recording me. Grandmama could be so cruel."

That old woman was so many things, and cruel was definitely high on the list. Curiosity finally got the better of me. "What did she record?" I asked.

Lila stared down at her hands. "It was after Luna's father died, when you and I were arguing about me not moving to Laguna Bay to raise Luna here. Grandmama caught me at a bad moment. She asked how things were going with you. With us."

She shook her head, pain etched across her face.

"I was tired," she whispered, "and angry." She swallowed hard.

My pulse thudded in my ears. I thought of things I'd said when I was tired and angry. Things I wished I could take back the instant they left my mouth.

"What did she record, sweetheart?" I asked.

Lila squeezed her eyes shut. Tears clung to her lashes. "I told her you were..." Her voice strained. "I told her you were a terrible mother. I told her you never wanted me, and that I wished I'd never been born."

For a second, I couldn't feel my fingers or anything. Only the echo of those words vibrating through me.

"She kept the recording on her phone," Lila added, once she found her voice again. "At first, she said it was to understand me better. For a while, I almost forgot about it. But when Luna was older, and we started talking about moving back here..." She swallowed. "She told me Luna could leave, but not me. She said if I tried, she'd send you that recording. She said she'd send it to everyone in Laguna Bay."

My mouth went dry.

A remarkable low even for Evangeline.

She wouldn't be content to rip my heart out. She'd wanted to humiliate me too.

But this wasn't about her hurting my pride.

This was about my daughter living under that threat for years.

"I'm so sorry you had to endure that," I said. "You should have let her do it. I'm a big girl. I could take it." Was that true? I wasn't entirely sure, but I would have done anything for Lila.

"Mom, I couldn't," she said. "I was so ashamed. I didn't mean it, but once she had the recording, I couldn't take it back."

I reached for her hand. It was cold and damp, her fingers stiff with tension. She didn't pull away.

"I was so young when I had you," I said. "I made mistakes. Letting you stay in New Orleans, especially after your father died, was one of my biggest. I told myself the Duvals were giving you a life I couldn't, but I should have known better. Of course you said things out of frustration. I probably earned a lot of them."

"No, you didn't," she said fiercely, looking up at me at last. Her eyes were still red, her lashes spiked with tears.

"That's the thing. You didn't. I know you tried your best. But she twisted it." She swallowed hard. "And I was so ashamed. I just didn't know how to tell you."

There it was—the bruise I could never see but had always sensed. All this time, I'd been certain I'd ruined her childhood in at least ten different ways. It never occurred to me she'd been carrying her own burdens.

"I knew if you ever heard that recording," Lila whispered, "you wouldn't love me anymore. I couldn't bear it."

The thought of my daughter believing that—that I could ever stop loving her—hurt more than any recording ever could have.

"You can't get rid of me that easily," I said, my throat thick.

A wet laugh burst out of her. She swiped under her nose with the back of her hand.

Lila swallowed hard. "Grandmama knew that was my fear. She even brought it up at the party to frighten me, right before her toast. I was so afraid she might do it right there in front of everyone. I panicked. That's why I threatened her." She buried her face in her hands.

That was the moment I'd seen. I remembered the confusion and distress on Lila's face. Now I knew why.

"When she collapsed," Lila continued, "I thought it was because of me. I thought I'd given her a heart attack."

I covered her hand with mine, trying to comfort her.

"But when they said it was poison, why didn't you say something then?"

She shook her head. "It just seemed too late. And what if they'd made a mistake? I didn't want to risk it."

"I wish I would have known," I said. "I wish I could have helped. I'm so sorry."

"You're helping now," she said. The words came out shaky but clear.

For a long moment neither of us spoke, then she said, "I love you. I know you did your best. I do."

I stared at her, my eyes stinging. "I love you too. More than anything. And for the record? You weren't wrong to be angry with me. I was a mess. But I never stopped trying. Not once."

"I know," she said.

Kheppy shifted closer, pressing her warm body against Lila's hip. "Humans say angry things when they are hurting," she said. "It does not erase the love they feel."

Lila let out a half-sniff, half-chuckle and stroked Kheppy's head. "All that wisdom in such an adorable, furry little package."

"I am adorable, aren't I?" Kheppy replied.

"And modest," I added with a smirk. "Don't forget modest."

We sat there for another minute, letting the quiet settle around us. The damp air cooled the heat in my cheeks.

Finally, I squeezed her hand and let go. "Come on," I said. "If we stay out here much longer, your aunt may send out a search party."

Lila sniffed and laughed again. "Can't have that."

She stood and brushed the dirt and dead leaves off the back of her jeans. I pushed myself up more slowly, my knees protesting the movement.

Kheppy hopped lightly down, and the three of us headed back toward the trail, moving side by side.

We were about halfway back to the house when Kheppy stopped so abruptly that I nearly tripped over her.

Her tail went rigid, fur bristling. Her ears flattened, angling toward the scrub lining the edge of the trail.

"Do you feel that?" she whispered.

"What?" Lila glanced around.

The air felt the same to me. Cold, damp, and carrying the lingering scents of wet grass and the distant sea.

But Kheppy's nose twitched, her eyes narrowing to slits.

"Someone is here," she said. "Not close, but getting closer."

An uncomfortable feeling slid down my spine, the kind that had nothing to do with the weather.

Lila inched closer. "Is it a werewolf?" she whispered.

"I don't think so," Kheppy said. "It's too far away to know for sure."

She turned to us, her tawny eyes serious. "Go to the house. Both of you. Quickly."

"Excuse me?" I said. "Since when do you give the orders?"

Kheppy didn't answer. Instead, she slipped behind a thick bush. There was the sound of rustling, a low thump, and then she returned as a sleek, silver-gray tiger. Her powerful shoulders rolled and stretched. Her stripes were darker than her usual tabby markings, but her eyes—those rich, molten-gold eyes—were exactly the same.

Lila grabbed my arm. "Mom," she whispered. "What is that?"

"That," I said, trying to remain calm, "is Kheppy's latest trick."

Kheppy—tiger-Kheppy—huffed, a soft chuffing sound that sent my pulse racing. She lowered her massive head, nudging us both from behind with gentle insistence toward the house.

"You have got to be kidding me," Lila breathed. "When did that start?"

"It's been an interesting few months," I said.

She looked at me, and despite everything, her mouth curved. "That sounds like an understatement."

We let Kheppy herd us down the trail, her bulk a solid presence at our backs. Every so often, she'd pause and look over her shoulder, scanning the shrubs and the boulders with a low growl rumbling in her chest. I didn't see anything, but the hair on my arms stood tall.

When we reached the gate, Kheppy stopped. She gave us one final nudge through the opening, then turned toward the wilderness again.

"Inside," she said, her voice deeper but still undeniably hers. "Lock the door. I will find the threat."

"Be careful," I said automatically, then caught myself. Was I really giving safety advice to a tiger?

She pinned me with her fiery gaze. "I am always careful."

Lila and I hurried across the yard. I didn't even complain about the splatters on my boots this time. At the back steps, I glanced over my shoulder.

Kheppy was already a blur on the hillside, a ripple of gray disappearing into the distance.

Lila tried to catch her breath. "Are things ever normal around here?"

"Depends on your definition of normal," I said.

I reached for the doorknob and squeezed her hand with my free one. "We're still standing. That's something."

It didn't feel like a happy ending. Not yet.

But as Lila and I stepped back into the warm, cluttered kitchen—and I slid the lock into place behind us—I felt, for the first time in a long while, like we'd finally knocked down the wall that had been standing between us.

Chapter 23

Ghostly Return

AT THE KITCHEN SINK, I stared out the window at the hills behind the house, trying to spot Kheppy in tiger form.

The sky dimmed by degrees as dusk settled in, and shadows stretched along the slope beyond the glass. Squinting, I searched for any sign of silver-gray fur in the distance.

Nothing.

The porch light clicked on automatically, spilling a soft yellow glow across the steps. A crow cawed and a motorcycle roared in the distance. Ordinary sounds that should have comforted me.

They didn't.

Behind me, the living room hummed with nervous energy. Chairs scraped softly as people shifted. A teaspoon clinked in a ceramic mug. No one was talking much, which was never a good sign in a house full of women who weren't usually this quiet.

"Kheppy wouldn't have shifted if she hadn't sensed trouble," I said, turning away from the window. "But I'm sure she knows what she's doing."

Was I fooling anyone? Probably not.

Delphine came up behind me. "We need to trust her," she said.

She meant I needed to trust Kheppy. She was right, of course, but it didn't make it any easier.

"What if the neighbor sees her?" I added. "I just wish she could have waited until it was dark. The last thing we need is for that woman to call the police or the fire department or even animal control about a loose tiger."

Delphine patted my back. "Let's hope it doesn't come to that. I'm going to make more tea."

"I'll take another cup if you're offering," Jemma said, moving to stand alongside Willa by the back door.

I held my post at the kitchen window while my sister fussed with the kettle. Opal stayed on the sofa, texting instructions to a neighbor who'd stepped in to watch her granddaughter.

"Has anyone heard from the Landon pack?" I asked, the question finally slipping free after circling my thoughts too long.

Willa gave me a sideways look. "You think the werewolves are prowling around out there?"

Jemma made a soft scoffing sound. "That was my thought too."

"Darren's been pressuring Sissy to get me involved," I said. "He wants me to persuade Howard to support their petition for a Midnight Council seat."

Jemma crossed her arms. "They're always up to something."

Willa shot her a look. "That's not very nice."

"Doesn't mean it isn't true," Jemma said.

"What are you suggesting?" Willa asked sharply.

I was curious too—but something moving outside caught my eye.

"There," I said, pointing to an outcropping of boulders and sage grass beyond the fence.

Kheppy emerged from the shadows and padded toward the porch. She was back in house cat form, her silver-gray fur catching what little light remained, her posture alert but unhurried.

Relief hit me so hard my knees nearly gave out.

I rushed out onto the porch before anyone could remind me it might not be safe.

"Well?" I asked as my feline friend reached the steps. "What happened?"

She didn't answer. Instead, she fixed her gaze on the empty space beside her.

Hadn't she heard me?

No, that wasn't it. She was looking at something.

Then I saw it. A shimmer so faint it was almost imperceptible.

My breath caught. "Is that what I think it is?"

Kheppy's eyes twinkled. "Not what. Who. It's Saphira."

Before I could ask how or why, Delphine stepped up beside me and offered her own greeting. "Saphira, my dear, it's so good of you to join us."

As far as I could tell, my sister was addressing what looked like thin air, but I wasn't about to point that out. I let her carry on.

"You have perfect timing," she continued, gently nudging me aside to make room for Kheppy and our invisible guest to come inside. "I've made a fresh pot of tea. You're probably not a tea drinker yourself—Kheppy isn't—but I'm sure we can find something to your liking. Unless..."

The look on my sister's face told me it had just dawned on her that ghost cats probably didn't drink anything at all.

As for me, I was starting to think I needed something stronger than caffeine.

A few minutes later, we regrouped in the living room with the electric lights turned low, at Kheppy's request. She insisted candlelight would help Saphira materialize.

With a little coaxing from Kheppy, it seemed to work. We all tried not to stare at the nearly translucent image of a Persian cat with the adorable pushed-in nose perched on the coffee table beside her.

Once everyone was settled, Kheppy coaxed her new friend forward. Saphira—her shape still fluid and faintly luminous—hesitated.

I decided to get things moving. "Saphira, what brought you here?"

Her spectral eyes went wide, a flash of distress passed through her fragile form, and then she snapped out of sight.

Kheppy frowned at me.

"What?" I asked. "It was just a question."

"You frighten her. It wasn't easy for her to come here," Kheppy said. "You must let her tell you what she has to say in her own way."

"Yes, Boo," Delphine added. "Have a little patience."

I sipped my tea. They knew—heck, everyone in this room knew—patience was not my forte.

Kheppy tilted her head toward what looked like empty space and murmured in a low, persuasive tone she reserved for the exceptionally stubborn, the overly dramatic, and—apparently—our scaredy-cat ghost.

A second later, the air rippled and Saphira drifted back into view, all wavy edges and soft, spectral glow.

As much as I wanted to speed up the process so we could find out why she had returned, I did my best to sit quietly, if not exactly patiently.

"Saphira is worried about Claire," Kheppy said.

Of course she was. The ghost cat had clearly been fond of Claire. If Claire had poisoned Evangeline on her behalf, as some kind of revenge, Saphira might even feel responsible. It could also explain Claire's argument with Howard, and why Willa had been working so hard to protect her.

"Saphira can't blame herself for Claire's actions," I said. "We all make our own choices."

Kheppy looked at me as if I were speaking gibberish. "Saphira says Claire did nothing worthy of blame."

I frowned. "Then why did the police take her in?"

Saphira opened her mouth, but no sound came out.

I squinted, then wiggled my fingers in my ears. "Sorry, I didn't catch that."

"I didn't either," Willa said.

The others murmured the same.

"Manifesting has strained her," Kheppy said. "As an unbound spirit, her ability to communicate is fading. It is easier for her to speak with me. I will try to translate. Give us a moment."

She conferred silently with Saphira, then nodded and turned back to the rest of us.

"She wants you to know the police were asking Claire about a different case—a different poisoning. Not Evangeline's," Kheppy said.

That got everyone's attention.

Kheppy explained that Detective Platt wanted to know about an incident that happened when Claire was in high school, and that the police were alerted by an anonymous tip called in after Evangeline's death. When they looked into it, they learned a teacher had been poisoned with foxglove at a high school in Claire's hometown decades ago, and Claire had been the prime suspect. The case never went to trial because Claire had been a minor.

"How is that anything more than an unfortunate coincidence?" I asked. "What makes the police think it has any connection to Evangeline's death?"

Kheppy spoke again with Saphira. When she turned back to us, she said, "When the police searched Claire's property, they found foxglove."

That seemed pretty circumstantial to me. But if I had to guess, the evidence Detective Platt was referring to when he released Lila—the evidence that was pointing the investigation in a different direction—probably related to foxglove being the poison that killed Evangeline. It was the only explanation that made sense.

I slanted a look at Willa. "Did you know about the incident with that teacher?"

She avoided my gaze.

"Willa," I pushed.

Fire ignited in her eyes. "The stigma of that incident followed her for years. She had to leave that town to get away from those false accusations."

"Were they false?" I asked.

She took a deep breath before continuing. "Claire's grandmother used to work in the school library. She knew that teacher. He was a piece of work. Every year, he forced his biology students to dissect rats."

I'd had to do the same. Judging by the others' faces, so had they.

"Only he didn't bring in rodent cadavers," Willa continued with disgust. "He brought in living animals, and he dispatched them himself. In front of the class."

The room went silent.

"Can you imagine?" Willa continued. "It was unspeakably cruel."

"I have to agree," I said finally. "I can understand Claire being upset and wanting to do something. But killing him wasn't the answer."

"She didn't kill anyone," Willa wailed. "That man is still very much alive. It wasn't a fatal dose."

"Fatal or not, she poisoned him," I said. "And now Evangeline? There's a pattern. That's what the police must think, anyway."

Willa froze. After a long pause, she shook her head. Slowly at first, then with increasing vigor. "Claire had nothing to do with it. With any of it."

"Of course she did," I said. "She must have slipped the foxglove into something Evangeline ate or drank."

Willa released a slow, measured breath.

No one moved.

"I know Claire didn't do it," she said with quiet determination, "because I did it."

Chapter 24
Too Close

No one moved.

Willa's confession didn't land with a bang. Instead, it seemed to suck the air out of the living room. Everyone froze. Delphine, Opal, Jemma, me—even Kheppy and our ghostly feline guest, Saphira.

"You can stop talking about Claire because she didn't do anything to Evangeline," Willa repeated, calm as could be. "I did. I poisoned that woman."

I stared at the tea cooling in my cup, latching onto it because my brain needed something ordinary. Something that made sense.

My instincts—annoying as they could be—were already whispering that something didn't add up.

I curled my fingers around my cup and reminded myself to breathe.

Across the room, Willa sat upright, hands folded in her lap, posture perfect. She didn't look wild-eyed or guilty. She looked resolved. Too resolved.

As Opal set her mug on the coffee table, her hand trembled, betraying her own doubts. Jemma and Lila stared into their laps, uncertain how to respond, and Delphine disappeared into the kitchen.

It was Jemma who spoke first.

"Willa," she said, "that took a lot of courage—"

"No," I snapped, before she could even finish the sentence. "It isn't..."

I stopped myself before I said *possible.*

Because it was always possible. People could always surprise you in horrible, inexplicable ways.

Even the ones you loved.

"I'm sure Willa had a good reason for doing what she did," Jemma said softly. "Evangeline was an awful woman who deserved what she got as far as I'm concerned."

My head snapped toward her, sending an angry pain shooting through my neck.

Jemma didn't look cruel or smug. She looked practical. Which somehow made it worse.

"Do you hear yourself?" I cried.

I squeezed my eyes shut and took a slow, calming breath, trying to soothe the hysteria swirling in my brain before I turned to Willa.

"Are you confessing because you did it?" I asked. "Or because you're trying to protect Claire?"

Jemma's eyes narrowed, and the corner of her mouth curled into something dangerously close to a sneer. I'd never seen that particular shade of anger on her before. "Maybe Willa did us a favor, Boo. Evangeline wanted the High Council to revoke our charter. She made that abundantly clear."

That heat. That venom. That wasn't like Jemma.

I felt something shift in the room.

And she wasn't finished. She gestured toward the cats. "And what she did to Saphira was unforgivable."

She met my gaze. "So, yes. I hear myself."

I sat there, absorbing what she'd said, and watching the others do the same.

I studied Willa again, searching for uncertainty or doubt.

There was none.

"I did what needed to be done," Willa said.

That was it. No apology. No details.

I swallowed hard. "So, you planned it? You prepared the foxglove poison and brought it to the party?"

Without hesitation, Willa said, "Yes."

One word.

"Then tell me how you did it," I said.

Her jaw tightened. "The powder was in my pocket. It was easy enough to slip it into her cup while she was distracted."

It should have been a relief to have clarity. Instead, it felt like my stomach dropped straight through the floor.

Opal leaned forward. "Willa," she whispered, as if saying her name with enough tenderness might unwind the confession, "are you sure you aren't confused? Perhaps you'd like to lie down."

"I don't need to lie down," Willa shot back. "And I'm not confused."

My heart ached for her, and my loyalty surged. We weren't just fellow gardeners, but friends who had weathered secrets, turmoil, and the constant churn of personal drama.

We stick together, no matter what. That's what she'd said.

Delphine reappeared in the doorway, drying her hands on a dish towel. She cleared her throat. "Why didn't you talk to us first?"

"Because you would have tried to stop me," Willa said.

There was no defensiveness in her voice. No drama. Just a simple statement of fact.

That, more than anything, shook me.

It frightened me even more than Willa's confession.

Delphine's mouth tightened. "What do we do now?"

"*We* don't do anything," Willa said. "I'm going to turn myself in. I just need to put my affairs in order, make arrangements for Pickles, and say goodbye to the little fella." Her fingers curled into fists in her lap, as if she were holding herself together by sheer force of will.

"Can we at least talk about this?" I asked.

She shot me a sharp look. "No," she said. "I've made up my mind."

Opal's voice softened. "We understand, but we care about you. We also know whatever you did, you must have had a good reason." She paused and glanced around. "It's getting late, and we could all probably benefit from a good night's sleep. Can we talk about it in the morning?"

"I don't think that'll be necessary," Willa said. "I've said all I have to say."

The room fell quiet. Then Willa stood and gathered her things.

None of us moved. Not because we wanted to let her leave, but none of us knew what to say or how to stop her.

When she went to the door, Jemma followed close behind. Opal lingered a beat, then joined them.

Delphine, Lila, and I watched their taillights disappear. As we went inside, Kheppy and Saphira moved toward the back door.

"Are you leaving too?" I asked.

I hadn't meant for it to sound so desperate. But after everything that had happened, I suppose I was feeling a little abandoned.

Kheppy paused, murmured something low to her ghostly friend, then crossed the room to stand in front of me. Tilting her head, she said, "Saphira needs me now, and I have questions for her. I'm curious about her experience of the afterlife."

The sincerity in her voice startled me.

My gaze shifted to Saphira, at the fragile shimmer of her outline.

Something about her made it impossible to look away.

"You know I would never refuse you anything," I said to Kheppy.

My companion's ears twitched. "I know. That's why I always return to you, and I always will."

I nodded, though my chest felt tight and full at the same time. "Please don't wander too far."

She brushed against my ankle in reassurance before turning back to Saphira, and the two of them slipped out into the night—one solid, one spectral—leaving the house quieter than it was before.

Lila let out a long breath once the three of us were alone. "Well. That was a lot."

"That's one way to put it," I said.

As Delphine, Lila, and I cleared away the dishes, I turned Willa's confession over in my mind.

"I can understand the impulse," I said. "The community was at risk, and Willa has always been one to sacrifice herself for the good of others."

Lila paused with a stack of plates in her hands. "But?"

"But I didn't see it coming," I finished. "How could I miss that?"

For all my confidence, all my instincts, I had to admit something uncomfortable: I might be too close to this.

"I think Opal was right," I said at last. "I think I could benefit from a good night's sleep."

Lila's mouth curved into a faint smile. "Good luck with that."

I rinsed the last mug and set it in the rack. The house felt different now, like it was holding its breath.

"I'll look at everything again in the morning," I said. "With a clear head."

Delphine hung her damp dish towel on the stove handle to dry and tapped my shoulder. "We'll figure it out. We always do."

I knew she was right.

Lila lingered nearby, watching me.

I looked at her, *really* looked at her, and felt something inside me loosen. I pulled her into a quick, gentle hug.

She rested her forehead against my shoulder for a heartbeat.

"We'll get through this," she murmured.

"We will," I said, trying to reassure her, even if I was still struggling to believe it myself.

Chapter 25

Cinnamon

I WOKE TO THE smell of cinnamon.

Not a hint of it, either. A rich blast that dragged me fully into the conscious world. For one blessed moment, I forgot about suspects, police stations, confessions, and the fact that our little supernatural community felt like it was teetering on the edge of a cliff.

Then reality returned—less like a crash and more like a thud—as I lay beneath my quilt, listening.

Laughter drifted down the hallway. Soft. Easy. Comforting.

When I finally rose and dressed, I followed the scent trail to the kitchen, where morning sunlight pooled across the linoleum like honey.

Delphine stood at the counter with flour on her cheek and her hair twisted into a loose knot, while Lila rolled out pie dough. There was an orange smear of pumpkin pie filling on the oven door, and a big bowl of it waiting nearby.

As I watched my sister and my daughter work, my mood lightened.

"You're up," Delphine said without turning around. "Perfect timing. We're baking."

"Looks like you're making a mess," I said, stepping to the cupboard to grab a mug.

"That too," Lila said. "There'll be plenty of time to clean up later."

"That's my girl," I murmured.

I leaned toward the mixing bowl and dipped a rebellious finger into the pumpkin filling.

A wooden spoon tapped my knuckles.

"Not ready," Delphine scolded, already steering me toward the cooling rack. She pressed a warm apple strudel muffin into my hand instead.

Not a bad trade-off.

Until I remembered who I was dealing with.

"Is this the real deal, or one of your vegan things?" I asked my sister.

She pretended to look offended.

"Vegan muffins are real muffins, but there's butter in there," she said. "We're also doing traditional pies, so I'm sure you'll be happy about that."

She was right. I was. The muffin's cinnamon-brown sugar topping crackled as I took a bite. Sweet streusel and tart apple melted together, and for a moment, everything felt right with the world.

Delphine wiped her hands on her apron. "Luna called this morning. She asked how many people we're expecting for Thanksgiving dinner tomorrow. She wants to know how many desserts to bring."

"You told her she doesn't have to go to any trouble, right?" I said. "We always have more than enough."

"Of course," she said, exchanging a glance with Lila. "She also asked if she could bring her new beau."

We knew Luna had been seeing someone, but we hadn't met him yet.

"What did you tell her?" I asked.

Delphine gave me a mischievous look. "I told her we'd be delighted to include him. But that means we'll need another chair. Merle took the extras from the party back to his place, didn't he? Could you swing by and pick one up on your way to the shop?" She smiled lightly. "Maybe a few. Just in case."

Considering our seating chart included the armchair's ottoman and the kitchen stool, it was probably a good idea.

"No problem," I said.

I didn't tell her I had already planned to head over to talk to him about Willa. Her confession had been sitting like a lump on my chest all night.

I fixed a travel mug full of strong tea and went to the door.

Kheppy was already there, perched on the window seat, her gray tail swaying beneath her as she watched the quiet street.

"Want to come along?" I asked.

She didn't turn her head. "I suppose."

On the drive, I glanced at her. "I missed you last night."

"Saphira and I had much to discuss."

I shifted my grip on the steering wheel. "Did she answer all your afterlife questions?"

"As well as she was able."

I was curious—more than I cared to admit—but this wasn't the moment.

As the silence stretched between us, my thoughts drifted back to more pressing matters: Claire in police custody, Willa dead set on confessing to a crime I didn't think she committed, and lingering questions about whether the werewolves had played a part in Evangeline's death.

As Merle's house came into view, so did Howard's pickup sitting out front.

That threw me.

I parked, grabbed Kheppy, and headed to the door, eager to find out why.

They were in the living room, huddled in conversation. Merle's shoulders were tense. Howard looked like he hadn't slept.

I hugged Kheppy closer. "What happened?"

"I was bringing Howard up to speed on Claire," Merle said.

"Have they arrested her?" I asked.

"Not yet. But I think it's only a matter of time," he said. "I was just telling Howard I was at the station earlier to check on my assignments, and I saw that Platt had left the case file open on his desk." He exhaled sharply. "I shouldn't have snooped, but I saw the toxicology report on the poison that killed Evangeline."

My heart dropped.

"And?" I asked.

He met my eyes. "It was digitalis."

In my world, digitalis was foxglove, and while it didn't exactly confirm Saphira's story, it came pretty close.

"Does it match the foxglove they collected from Claire's property?" I asked.

Merle frowned. "How do you know about that?"

I filled him and Howard in on the ghost cat's story.

"I suppose they could match it with more tests," he said, "but I didn't see anything in the report that mentioned a source." He thought for a moment, then added, "Even if they trace the foxglove to a particular site, I think you also have to consider who had access." He cocked his head to the side. "Frankly, I'm a little surprised by your reaction. You seem pretty convinced Claire's guilty based on something that looks like circumstantial evidence at best."

He was absolutely right. I was trying to protect Willa at Claire's expense.

"I'm sorry," I said, trying to backpedal. "It's just that last night, Willa told us she killed Evangeline, and she's planning to turn herself in this morning."

Both men froze.

Howard rubbed his face in disbelief. "She did what now?"

"She confessed. She said she did it, but I'm having a hard time believing it."

I turned to Merle. "I have to assume she hasn't followed through with it yet, or you would have heard about it when you were down there. My guess is she's still sorting out what to do with Pickles."

Howard still appeared to be in shock. "She's trying to protect Claire."

"That's my guess too," I said. "But it's only a guess. Either that, or she's protecting the community. You know Willa."

"I do know Willa," Howard said. "And she's definitely doing it to protect Claire."

The way he said it wasn't speculation. It was fact.

"You know something, don't you?" I said.

He looked at Merle, then back at me. For a long moment, he said nothing. Then it burst out of him in a rush. "She did something a long time ago, and she's never forgiven herself. It was rash. Impulsive."

The room seemed to tilt. Something in my brain clicked.

"Did it involve a high school biology teacher?" I demanded.

It had been a guess, but the look on Howard's face confirmed it.

"Willa doesn't know that I know," he added quickly, almost apologetically. "It's something I sort of..."

"Intuited?" I asked, giving a euphemistic name to his psychic ability.

He nodded.

"I never said anything because it's a painful memory for her," Howard said. "When she did it, she had no idea how it would affect Claire, and she's felt guilty about it ever since. That's why she's gone out of her way to help Claire settle here. Willa would do anything to protect that woman. It's her way of making amends."

That had to explain the vague, undefined feeling in my gut.

Relief rushed through me. "I need to talk to Willa before this goes too far," I said.

I checked the clock. If she hadn't turned herself in yet, there was a good chance she was sticking to her regular morning routine, which was largely determined by Pickles' walking and eating schedule. But I was already cutting it close.

"I'm going to head over to Willa's and see if I can catch her before it's too late," I said.

"Want backup?" Merle asked, a hopeful edge in his voice.

He wanted to help. And part of me wanted him beside me.

But Willa and I shared a history. The group talk the night before hadn't worked, but maybe one-on-one, I could make her see reason.

"I don't want it to look like we're ganging up on her," I said. "Besides, I was hoping you might take a few folding chairs to my place for Delphine for tomorrow."

He grimaced, clearly aware that folding chairs were not a high priority.

"Of course," he said. "If you're sure."

"I think it's for the best."

Outside, the sky hung low and gray. The air felt still, like the whole world was on hold.

As I slid behind the wheel, all the questions that had been tumbling through me on the drive over fell away. What remained was my concern for Willa. Was she on a suicide mission to right an old wrong?

Or was she sacrificing herself to protect our community?

My thoughts circled those possibilities, getting me nowhere.

Right now, the only thing that mattered more than getting answers was reaching my friend before she made a terrible mistake.

Chapter 26

Voice of Reason

THE MIDMORNING DRIVE TO Willa's yellow cottage felt shorter than it should have.

I'd left Merle's place certain—righteously certain—that Willa couldn't have poisoned Evangeline. I'd convinced myself she was sacrificing herself for Claire, acting out of lingering guilt tied to what she'd done to a biology teacher years ago.

But as I turned onto Willa's quiet street, new doubts crept in.

What if I were wrong?

My instincts had been off before.

And if she had killed Evangeline, could I really blame her?

That last thought unsettled me more than I cared to admit. My ex-mother-in-law hadn't exactly charmed Laguna Bay. She'd swept in with threats and insults, leaving nothing but tension in her wake. If Willa truly believed she was protecting Claire—or even the rest of us—did that make it murder or something more complicated?

I tightened my grip on the steering wheel.

"No, that's not how we do things," I muttered.

Kheppy glanced over from the passenger seat. "You're talking to yourself again."

"I'm processing."

The look she gave me said she knew better, but she let it go.

As I turned the corner, Willa's front garden came into view, sunlight catching the lavender, hibiscus, and hydrangeas, setting them aglow. The color was so vivid, I nearly missed Jemma's familiar silver minivan parked nearby.

"Oh, thank goodness," I said. It meant Willa was still home.

It also meant I wouldn't have to talk her out of turning herself in by myself. I'd told Merle I wanted to handle this one-on-one, but having Jemma there was probably for the best.

Kheppy shot me a questioning look.

"You think Willa will welcome this intervention?"

"Guess we're about to find out," I said.

I parked along the curb in front of the house and cut the engine.

"Are you coming?" I asked.

Kheppy wrapped herself into a cozy ball on the passenger seat before responding. "I'll wait here."

"Suit yourself."

As I approached the front door, I wondered what had changed Jemma's mind. Yesterday, she'd been so quick to accept Willa's guilt. Had she regretted that? Or was she simply here out of solidarity?

Either way, I was glad I wouldn't have to face this moment alone.

I knocked. When no one answered, I rang the bell and waited.

Still nothing.

That was odd.

Instead of knocking again, I circled around the side of the house.

The gravel crunched beneath my boots as I rounded the corner. I glanced back toward the street and noticed Kheppy had lifted her head to watch me. Our eyes met for the briefest moment. She cocked her head to the side, curious, then settled back down.

When I reached the back of the house, I spotted Willa through the window, sitting at the counter, sipping tea and talking with Jemma. I waved, lifting my hand high enough to catch their attention.

For a second, I was sure Jemma saw me. Her eyes darted toward the window—sharp and assessing—before she deliberately turned away.

I stood there, dumbfounded. Confused for a second, then angry.

Was Jemma seriously brushing me off?

If she thought I'd take the hint and leave, she didn't know me very well.

Luckily, Willa noticed me, her expression shifting quickly from concentration to surprise. She hurried to the back door and opened it.

"Boo? What are you doing here?"

"I tried knocking, but no one answered. Should I take it personally?" I asked casually as I stepped into the kitchen, which smelled of chamomile tea and fresh bread. An adorable set of giant ceramic mugs shaped like Pickles' adorable face sat on the counter, steam curling upward.

Willa touched her ear and shook her head. "Sorry about that, dear," she said. "I seem to have misplaced my hearing aid. Jemma was helping me look for it, but then we got sidetracked with tea and Pickles, and one thing and another. We're going over Pickles' regimen. She'll be taking care of him while I'm away."

She didn't say the word, but it settled over the room all the same. Prison.

"I was wondering who would take care of him," I said. "I'm glad he'll be in good hands."

Guess the reason for Jemma's visit wasn't to talk our friend out of confessing after all.

I tried to catch Jemma's eye, but she refused to look at me, preferring to study her fingernails instead.

My gaze drifted toward the swinging door to the dining room. Something felt off. Too quiet. "Where is Pickles?"

"I put him in his room to calm down," Willa murmured, almost embarrassed. "He wasn't behaving himself."

"He'll be fine," Jemma reassured her. "Don't worry about a thing."

"I just don't know what got into him," Willa said, shaking her head. "He never nips like that."

"I'm sure it's nothing," Jemma said in a soothing voice. "Too much excitement."

Pickles nipped? Pickles never nipped.

Willa's smile trembled at the edges.

"He can probably sense that you'll be leaving," I said.

I wasn't above using Pickles' well-being as leverage.

"Can we talk about it?" I pressed.

The kindly smile on Willa's face vanished. "Nothing to talk about."

"There's everything to talk about," I shot back.

I'd hoped to see something in Willa's expression that would tell me she was having second thoughts about turning herself in, but she looked as resolute as ever.

Willa straightened, sitting tall and rigid. "I made my decision."

"And it's a brave one," Jemma said softly.

I shot her a look. Whose side was she on?

Willa rose and smoothed her heather-gray sweater, bulky and at least two sizes too big for her petite frame. "I'm going to check on Pickles," she said. "See if he's calmed down."

She went to the swinging door, and I followed. Behind us, Jemma gathered the cups onto a tray—adding an extra one, presumably for me—and carried them to the dining room table, where sunlight filtered across the lace runner and caught the edge of the china cabinet.

As I stepped into the dining room, something small and white caught my eye from the planter beside the window.

I paused, then reached in and pulled out a tiny hearing aid.

"Willa," I said, just as she returned with Pickles tucked under her arm, "is this yours?"

She frowned. "Oh—yes. Where did you find it?"

"In the planter."

Her brows knit together. "How would it get there?"

I was wondering the same thing. Willa wouldn't have put it there. Was she getting forgetful? Or was it something else?

But the hearing aid wasn't why I was here.

"Willa," I said as she set Pickles down and motioned for me to sit beside her at the table, "have you thought this through?"

I braced for an angry outburst, but she just sighed.

"For the last time," she said, watching Pickles circle her legs, "yes. I have."

I waited while Jemma poured the tea, the soft clink of porcelain filling the silence, then tried again.

"If you're doing it to protect Claire, I'm sure she would prefer you didn't."

Willa's gaze darted, not to me, but to Jemma.

Just for a second.

"Some people deserve a second chance," she said.

Jemma lifted the teapot and peered inside. "I should probably make a fresh pot," she said lightly and disappeared back into the kitchen.

Coward.

Silence settled over the room, broken only by the ticking clock as Pickles ran in circles, chasing his own squiggly tail.

Then he trotted toward the kitchen, his tiny claws clicking rapidly across the tile as he went in search of something that had caught his attention. A moment later, I heard the familiar slurp of water at the back door.

Now that Willa and I were alone, I searched for a diplomatic way to bring it up again.

I found none.

"I won't let you do this," I said.

Willa didn't even blink. "It isn't up to you."

As much as I hated to admit it, she was right. I couldn't force her to do anything. It was her choice, and there was nothing I could do about it.

At least nothing I could think of at the moment.

"I should help with the tea," I said because I needed a minute. Needed space to think.

I pushed through the swinging door into the kitchen just as Jemma tipped the last of a fine white powder from a small glass vial into the sugar bowl on the counter.

She hadn't heard me.

The kettle hissed on the stove, masking the soft tap of the bowl's lid as she replaced it.

"What is that?" I asked.

Jemma froze.

Then, slowly, she turned to me.

"Just sugar," she said evenly.

"I thought you were making tea."

For a moment, I thought she might laugh it off. Brush it aside. Tell me I was being ridiculous.

I moved closer.

"Jemma?"

She pushed the empty vial toward the sink as if it were nothing.

I reached past her and grabbed it.

"Jemma..."

Fine white granules clung to the inside. I hadn't seen foxglove powder in years, but I had no doubt that was what I was looking at. What I didn't understand was why.

The warmth drained from her expression. What replaced it wasn't panic.

It was calculation.

"You shouldn't have come in here," she said. "You shouldn't have come here at all."

"It was you?" The question slipped out, stunned.

Slowly, it was dawning on me.

She hadn't come here to help Willa or to care for Pickles.

She'd come to plant evidence. To be sure the blame stuck once Willa confessed.

I understood that just in time to see her reach for the knife.

And feel it press into my side.

Chapter 27
Sugar Bowl

THE KNIFE'S TIP PRESSED into my back as Jemma pushed me through the swinging door into the dining room.

One wrong move, and that knife would slice right through my skin.

Willa looked up from the table. "We've wasted enough time. Will one of you take me to the station, or do I need to call a rideshare?"

Practical as ever. As if she were heading out to run errands.

Jemma nudged me toward a chair. "Sit, Boo. And you're not going anywhere, Willa. Not yet."

"I told you," Willa said, impatience creeping into her voice, "I've made up—"

She stopped short.

Her gaze dropped to the knife.

"What's going on?" she demanded.

"I tried it the easy way," Jemma said. "But Boo couldn't help herself."

The color drained from Willa's face.

"You don't have to do this," she said quickly. "When I turn myself in and confess, it'll be over. You won't have anything to worry about."

The words hit me like a slap across the face.

"You can't make her do this," I said over my shoulder to Jemma.

Willa shook her head. "She isn't, Boo. It's my choice."

I stared at her, trying to understand.

Jemma let out a brittle laugh. "It's too late for that now, Willa. It might have worked if Boo hadn't started asking questions."

I rubbed my temples, trying to make sense of what I was hearing. Piecing it all together. "So it was you, Jemma? You killed Evangeline and were going to let Willa take the blame? Then why plant evidence in her kitchen?"

I waited for Jemma to answer. This woman I'd considered a friend. No, more than that. She was practically family.

And now she was threatening us with a chef's knife.

"A confession could fall apart under cross-examination," Jemma said. "But evidence won't. I had to be sure."

Willa scoffed. "Is that why you called in the tip about Claire? You were going to try to blame her? You were the only one I ever told about that teacher."

Jemma shrugged. "I was trying to save you. But you couldn't even see that."

"I never asked you to do that," Willa said. "Now she'll face the same scandal she faced up north. It'll start all over again."

I turned to Willa. "You did the same thing. You threw suspicion on the council elders and the werewolves when you knew it was Jemma." That betrayal cut deep.

"No, I didn't know she'd done it. Not then," she said. "At least not for sure. Jemma told me after you talked to the elders." The memory weighed heavily on her.

I considered keeping the secret Howard had shared with me, but keeping secrets had caused too much trouble already. "Howard told me what happened with Claire," I said. "About what happened with her biology teacher. I understand why you've been watching out for her and why you didn't say anything about knowing her before."

Willa went pale. "How does he know?"

The shock lingered for a moment, but then her composure slid back into place.

"Of course he knows. His powers have always been more powerful than he lets on," she said more quietly, the realization dawning on her. "He's just been too kind to say anything."

She drew in a deep breath, her shoulders squaring as she regained control.

Jemma had no interest in talking. She shoved us into chairs, then, with a swift slice of the knife, cut the cord that held the drapes. Never loosening her grip on the blade, she used the cord to bind my wrists to the chair arms with unsettling efficiency.

While she worked, Willa edged toward the door. Jemma's gaze snapped to her. "Don't," she said. "I don't want to hurt you, but I will if you make me."

Jemma tugged the knots tight, like she'd done this before. The coarse fiber scraped against my skin, leaving a sting that bloomed hot and immediate.

"There," she said, stepping back to assess her work before slicing off the remaining length of cord and moving on to Willa.

"Jemma," I said carefully, "you don't have to do this."

"You shouldn't have gotten involved," she said. "I had it all worked out. But you always have to meddle," she added with a scowl that could have scorched paint. "I had it all planned. You weren't supposed to be part of it."

"But why?" I asked. "Why did you have to kill Evangeline?"

"She deserved it," she said bluntly.

"Because of the charter?" I shook my head. "She was awful, yes. I know that better than anyone. Maybe we could have reasoned with her."

Jemma leaned back against Willa's hutch, her collection of teacups rattling lightly behind her.

"There's no reasoning with a woman like that," she said. "And you have no idea what she did to me. No one does. Except Willa."

When I looked at Willa, she glanced away.

There was more to that story. Another secret.

"Tell me," I said.

"I told you I had a florist business before the gelato shop. Did you know it was in New Orleans?" she asked, an acidic edge creeping into her voice.

I shook my head.

Had she ever mentioned that? I was sure I would've remembered.

As she spoke, I slowly twisted my wrists against the cord. It bit deeper into my skin—but there. The faintest give.

Something.

"That shop was my dream," Jemma went on. "A little place near the French Market in the Quarter. It was thriving, until Evangeline decided a friend of hers wanted the space."

There it was.

The thread that tied her to Evangeline Duval.

"Suppliers vanished. Customers disappeared. Rumors spread. Just like that, sales dried up."

The fibers bit into my skin as I twisted my wrists.

Don't stop talking.

"I lost everything. Moved back to Colorado. Had to live with my parents for three years to recover."

Her jaw tightened.

"She had the audacity to smile to my face," Jemma said, her voice dropping cold, "and call it business."

The knot cinched tighter as I worked to free myself.

"I'm so sorry," I said.

"I thought I was over it," Jemma said. "I told myself I'd moved on. But then you announced she was coming here with your daughter, and I knew I had to do something. I had to make her pay."

"What did you do?" I asked. I had to keep her talking. As long as she was talking, she wasn't hurting Willa, and I had time to work the knots loose.

"I knew about the foxglove at Claire's place," she continued. "It was easy to snip some and prepare the powder. Every garden witch does, right?" She half-chuckled. It was almost like it was a relief for her to get the story off her chest. Like she was proud of it.

"I brought it with me to the party, but I almost had a change of heart. All that worrying about how I'd do it, it actually did make me a little queasy." She turned to me then. "But then you poured that glass of lemonade, and it was the perfect opportunity. No one was around. Everyone was outside."

I remembered leaving the lemonade on the counter when I'd gone to get her medicine.

"But that's not who we are," I said, stalling for time. "We value life. We protect it."

She shrugged. "I didn't ask Willa to confess. She offered."

I turned to my friend. "Is that true?"

She nodded.

"Why?"

"When Jemma told me what she'd done, I couldn't bear the thought of her going to prison," Willa said. "Not after what that woman put her through."

"That's very noble," I said. "But what about you? You shouldn't have to pay for something you didn't do."

Willa's calm only made me more frantic, but the loop I'd been tugging was finally giving way. I forced my breathing to slow. I couldn't let Jemma see my excitement.

"Revenge," I said gently, "won't right the wrong that was done to you."

Jemma's expression hardened. "Spare me."

I gave the cord one final, careful twist.

My right hand slipped free.

I didn't move.

Not yet.

Her attention shifted back to Willa, who sat bound and pale.

"We'll figure this out," Jemma muttered.

That was my moment.

I lunged.

The chair tipped, scraping loudly against hardwood. The knife skidded across the floor—but she grabbed it before I could reach it.

Jemma was stronger than she looked.

She twisted, shoved me hard, and scrambled to her feet.

Before I could recover, she hooked her arm around Willa's neck and pressed the blade against her throat.

"Enough!" Jemma shouted.

I froze.

The world narrowed to the thin line of steel against Willa's skin.

"Don't," I begged, holding up my free hand.

My heart pounded so loudly I could hear it in my ears.

I scanned the room for something—anything—to throw. A teapot. A bookend. A candlestick.

"Go ahead," Jemma mocked. "Try it."

I stilled.

This wasn't about pride. It was about keeping Willa safe.

And then—

A clatter from the kitchen, and then Pickles' frantic yapping.

All three of us went still.

From beyond the swinging door came a deep, familiar voice.

"Boo? Are you here? I brought the police."

Merle.

Relief hit me so hard, it left me dizzy.

Jemma's confidence cracked.

Her grip loosened—just enough to turn—

That was my moment.

I reached for the nearest thing—the handle of a giant Pickles mug.

Jemma pivoted at the sound, but not fast enough.

I swung.

The impact vibrated up my arm and rang through the room like a bell struck hard.

She crumpled.

The knife clattered across the floor.

Silence followed. Thick. Absolute. Broken by the sudden and repeated yips of Pickles from deep in the kitchen.

I stood there, trying to catch my breath. "Merle?" I called.

No answer.

Instead, a small, dignified figure sauntered through the swinging door.

Kheppy.

Her tail was high. Her amber eyes gleamed.

"That was you?" I asked, stunned.

"I thought you were taking too long, so I came in through Pickles' doggy door."

That explained the yapping.

"I heard what was happening," Kheppy continued, "and thought you might need Merle's assistance."

"So you mimicked him?" I asked.

"I did," she added.

A shaky laugh escaped me as I scooped up the fallen knife and put it safely on the counter. I rushed to Willa to be sure she was all right.

Once I knew she was, I moved on to Jemma. Her pulse was strong. Her breathing steady.

Then I grabbed my phone.

Several minutes later, sirens wailed in the distance—growing louder, closer—until three police cruisers screeched to a halt in front of the house.

Boots pounded across the porch.

Uniformed officers flooded inside, weapons drawn and voices sharp with commands. Behind them—thank goodness—was Detective Platt.

"You've been busy, Ms. Boudreaux," he said dryly.

I exhaled. "How many times do I have to say it? It's just Boo."

After he hauled Jemma to her feet, turned her over to the officers, and directed them to the foxglove powder I'd alerted him to in Willa's sugar bowl, I gave him a version of events I hoped would hold up under legal scrutiny and keep the secrets of Laguna Bay's supernatural community:

When I'd caught Jemma planting evidence to frame Willa, she'd panicked.

We'd struggled.

I'd defended myself.

All of it technically true.

The detective's eyes lingered on me a fraction longer than necessary, and I had the distinct impression he knew there was more to the story. All he said was, "One of these days, you and I are going to have a long talk about why you keep finding yourself at crime scenes."

He might have pressed for more information, but Merle stepped in.

"Sorry to interrupt, Detective," Merle said. "I just wanted to let Boo know we found her cat out back."

He met my gaze and held it. "I know you were worried."

There was something deliberate in his expression.

I nodded slowly. "I appreciate that, Merle. Thank you."

The detective studied us both, then glanced down at his notepad. "We'll need you down at the station later for a formal statement, but this should do for now. I'd like to check on Ms. Wendall, anyway." He hesitated, then added, "I hope your cat's all right."

"Thank you," I said. "I hope so too."

As he moved toward Willa and the paramedic crouched beside her, Merle and I slipped out the back door.

The cold air hit my lungs like clarity.

Once we were safely out of normie earshot, I turned to him. "What do you mean you found Kheppy?"

He gave a small, almost sheepish shrug. "I needed a reason to get you out of there."

I'd suspected as much—but for one awful second, I'd feared a tiger-sized Kheppy might be wandering the yard.

"You scared me," he said quietly as we walked.

"I scared myself."

He reached for my hand, careful of the cord burns on my wrists. His palm was warm against the chill.

"You were good in there," he murmured.

Across the yard, paramedics wheeled Willa toward the ambulance. She caught sight of me and lifted a trembling hand.

"Feed Pickles, will you?"

"Of course," I called. "I'll take care of him. Don't worry. I'll come see you soon."

She waved it off like it wasn't necessary.

It was.

She'd been through more than anyone should in one afternoon. And for a moment in that kitchen, I'd almost lost her.

Merle's fingers tightened around mine. "You want to ride with her, don't you?"

If I didn't know ghost-whispering was his special talent, I'd suspect he was a mind reader.

"I have to take care of Pickles," I reminded him.

"I know where she keeps the kibble," he said. "And I can hang around until the emergency people leave, and make sure no one pokes into places they shouldn't."

There wasn't much they'd find that screamed garden witch. Plenty of perfectly ordinary Laguna Bay residents owned herbal teas and essential oils.

Still.

"You don't mind?" I asked, searching his face.

Those big, earnest blue eyes didn't waver.

Then I felt it—a soft brush of kitty fur against my ankle.

Kheppy.

I bent and scooped her up. "Where'd you run off to?"

"That dog wouldn't leave me alone," she said, clearly unimpressed. "I needed distance."

I couldn't blame her. Pickles seemed to have taken a liking to her.

Merle stepped closer. "I saw your purse inside. I'll grab it so you can get going."

He didn't wait for more than a nod before heading back to the house, and I knew he was giving me a moment with Kheppy. He was thoughtful that way.

"It's a good thing you showed up when you did," I said, holding her close so no one else would hear. "Thank you."

"You were in danger," she murmured. "I had to act."

Then, more quietly, "She deceived me as well. I should have sensed it."

I stilled. "Kheppy—"

"My instincts were off," she admitted, the words clearly costing her. "I do not like that."

"She fooled all of us, sweetheart," I said gently.

But there was something I needed to understand. "Why impersonate Merle? Why not take your tiger form?"

"A tiger would have created chaos, and that could have put you in more danger," she said. "Jemma might have panicked and lashed out. With Merle, she would be disoriented, but not reckless."

Whatever the reasoning, her plan had worked.

I pressed my cheek to the top of her head, feeling the tension loosen with each breath.

For weeks, I'd been fighting—for my daughter, for this town, for a version of the truth that didn't tear everything apart.

Today, I'd fought for everything I loved.

And that felt... different.

Stronger.

Thanksgiving was tomorrow. There would be a feast to prepare, candles to light, and people to embrace.

But as the police cruiser pulled away with Jemma in the back seat, red and blue lights flashing against the gray afternoon sky, another realization settled in.

I didn't have to brace for what came next.

For the first time since Evangeline Duval collapsed in my backyard, I felt ready.

Not just grateful, but at peace.

I drew in a slow breath of cold, clean air.

Tomorrow, we would give thanks.

Today, we survived.

Chapter 28

Feast

DELPHINE AND OPAL HAD taken over the kitchen. There were checklists, diagrams, and schedules. Stacks of platters, bowls, and serving ware that only came out for the very best occasions.

I offered to help because I'm not completely useless. Delphine pressed a basket into my hands and said, "Take Lila. Go pick something in the garden to decorate the table."

Opal had brought a darling centerpiece, but I figured it was easier to follow directions than argue. Besides, it would give Lila and me a chance to talk. She'd gotten a call from the Duval estate lawyer the night before, and now that the police had arrested Jemma for Evangeline's murder and cleared her, she had to fly back to New Orleans in the morning to meet with him.

Lila and I pulled on jackets and trudged outside to gather sprigs of eucalyptus and whatever blooms I could find to add to Opal's already impressive bouquet. Kheppy joined us to supervise the harvest.

"I wish you didn't have to go back so soon," I said, keeping my voice light. "I thought we would have more time together."

"Me too." She snipped a vibrant hydrangea. "I still can't believe she left me everything. She never said she was going to do that."

Evangeline Duval had spent years controlling my daughter's life. And now, with one legal document, she seemed to want to keep doing it from beyond the grave.

Of course she did.

"But now you're in control," I said. "I'm here if you need me, but I think you've got this."

Lila nodded.

I looked down at the basket—at the tidy collection we'd gathered for a table that was about to overflow with food and people we held dear.

My gaze drifted to a patch of calendula near the edge of the garden. Bright orange blooms dotted the plant, stubborn and cheerful. They had usually faded this late in the season.

I crouched and touched one petal. Soft and velvety.

"These are usually dormant by now," I murmured.

Lila glanced down. "Has Delphine been whispering to the plants again?"

"Delphine whispers to everything," I said.

It earned a laugh that cheered us both.

I clipped the calendula anyway and tucked the blooms into the basket.

"I'm not worried about your ability," I said. "I'm worried about what going back to New Orleans might do to you."

Her throat bobbed. "I can do it," she said.

I sensed a strength within her I hadn't heard before. I hesitated, then went for the question I'd been holding back. "Are you ever going to tell Luna about it? I mean, all of it?"

The clatter of Delphine in the kitchen drifted faintly through the back door—metal clinking and someone laughing.

Lila looked down at the flowers, not at me. "Luna's smart," she said carefully. "She already knows some of it."

"Some of it," I echoed.

"She knows there's more to this life than aromatherapy and tarot cards." Lila's mouth twisted.

"Of course she does. And we've always been careful around her. Even Kheppy." Our supernatural friends embraced Luna, but everyone understood the same unspoken rule: Luna only knew so much.

Lila exhaled and finally met my eyes. "I appreciate that. I do. And I will tell her. But not today."

I didn't push. Not because I didn't want the truth out in the open, but because Lila deserved to do it in her own time and in her own way.

"Someday," Lila added, almost like a promise.

Kheppy stepped up onto the low stone border near the lavender and gazed at Lila.

"Someday is what humans say when they're stalling," Kheppy said.

Lila's lips parted in surprise. Then she smiled. "I suppose you're right, Kheppy."

Kheppy's tail swished. "Of course I am."

"Oh, my sweet little friend, you do have a way with words." I ran my fingers over her head.

Lila chuckled softly.

"I'm so glad you came," I said before I could overthink it. "I hope you know that."

The words felt simple. True. And long overdue.

Her eyes went glossy, and she covered it by reaching for another hydrangea bloom. Then her hand came up instead and rested on my shoulder.

"Me too, Mom," she said.

For a moment, we stood like that, the garden air and the weight of difficult years between us softening into something gentler.

The click of the side gate's metal latch broke the silence.

Willa stepped into view, a fresh white bandage peeking over the cowl of her copper sweater. Another wrapped around her left wrist. She still looked a little shaken around the edges, but steadier than she had yesterday. In the crook of her right arm, like a furry, wrinkled loaf of bread, was Pickles.

"I hope you don't mind that I brought him," Willa said as Pickles wiggled and emitted a tiny snort. "He and

Kheppy seemed to get along yesterday, and after the troubles, it didn't feel right leaving him home alone."

I stepped forward and scratched the little guy between the ears.

"Of course we don't mind," I said. "Pickles is family too. Isn't that right, Kheppy?"

Kheppy stared at the dog for a moment, then said, "Yes, of course. If you need me, I'll be inside." She turned and trotted toward the back door.

Willa watched her go, then gave me an apologetic look.

"She'll warm up to him," I assured her. "I think we're all still recovering from yesterday. Honestly, I wasn't sure I'd be up to socializing today. I'm surprised you are. Did you drive? You should have called. I would've picked you up."

"I didn't want to bother you, and I feel fine," she said. "Just a few bumps and scratches. The bruised ego is the worst of it. I can't help feeling foolish. Betrayed even. I should have seen what Jemma was doing—"

"No." I stepped in and wrapped my arms around her, probably less gently than I should have, given the bandages and Pickles.

Willa stiffened in surprise, then let out a soft, breathy laugh as Pickles yipped between us.

"None of it was your fault," I said hoarsely as I pulled back. "You have a big heart. Don't ever apologize for that."

She cradled Pickles more tightly to comfort him, then smiled sheepishly at me. "I hope you won't mind when I tell you I made a last-minute invite. I ran it by Delphine, but I probably should have run it by you as well."

That got my full attention.

Willa opened her mouth as Claire appeared at the side of the house.

"Happy Thanksgiving," she said with a hesitant smile. "I brought dessert. Willa told me you like cherry cobbler."

She lifted a foil-covered pan.

It took me a second to find my footing. Then I realized the truth—Claire was here, and I was okay with that. More than okay.

"That's a dangerous thing to bring into my house," I said, smiling despite myself. "I have very little self-control around a good cobbler."

Willa shifted and whispered before Claire reached us. "She didn't have anyone local to spend the holiday with, and after everything, well, I thought it might be nice. I hope you don't mind."

I exhaled slowly. "Not in the least."

As Claire joined us, her shoulders dropped. "It's so good of you to include me at the last minute like this," she said. "Willa said it wouldn't be any trouble. I hope that's true."

"No trouble at all," I told her. "Is Saphira with you?"

Claire's smile softened. Her gaze darted to the corner near the avocado tree, as if she half-expected to see a ghostly shimmer in the shade.

"I haven't seen Saphira since I got home," she admitted. "But she knows she's welcome to stay with me, if she wants. Something tells me I'll see her again. Or maybe that's just wishful thinking."

Pickles chose that moment to demand freedom. Willa set him down, and he waddled off with purpose.

The back door swung open, and Delphine leaned out. "Turkey's ready!"

"On our way," I called back.

Lila glanced down at our collection of eucalyptus and flowers. "Guess she doesn't need these after all."

I arched an eyebrow. "I think you're right."

We filed inside—Claire balancing her cobbler, Willa wrangling Pickles like a grumpy toddler, Lila carrying the basket of flowers—and found the living room completely transformed. A long, covered table stretched across the center, chairs pulled neatly into place all around it.

My stomach gave an impatient growl, making it clear it hadn't entirely forgiven me for yesterday's stress. At the smell of turkey, sage, and the bright tang of cranberry, it did seem willing to negotiate if the portions were generous.

In the entryway, Luna and her boyfriend—or was it fiancé? I genuinely couldn't keep up—were taking off their coats.

Luna, her corkscrew curls fanning over her shoulders, turned as we entered the living room.

"Mom," she said when she spotted Lila, and that one word carried a whole history of complicated love, "I want to introduce you to someone."

Lila went to her immediately, her face beaming in a way I hadn't seen in years. She reached out and touched Luna's cheek like she needed proof she was real.

I stood there for a moment, watching them, transfixed by the moment.

I probably would have stood there all day if Merle hadn't come up beside me. He'd been standing nearby with Howard, keeping watch as the parade of steaming dishes were delivered by the kitchen crew. Mashed potatoes. Gravy. Green beans. Even Delphine's vegan dishes looked suspiciously appetizing.

On a platter near the center of the table sat something shaped like a small turkey.

It was not a turkey.

"Is that tofu?" I asked Delphine as she passed.

"Try it," she said without stopping. "You might like it."

We both knew I wasn't going to try it.

Merle must have heard the exchange because I caught him snickering behind his hand. He was in a button-down shirt that made him look annoyingly handsome and heartbreakingly rested, considering the week we'd had.

"Delphine put you over here by me," I said, tapping a chair. "I hope your plus-one doesn't mind that he won't get a seat. It's a full house today."

"That's all right," he said. "Rupert isn't here."

"Really?" That was new. Merle and his ghostly BFF were usually inseparable.

"Really," he said, like it meant something.

Considering how much his spirit companion had come between us over the years, it did.

I swallowed the sudden thickness in my throat and nodded. "Good."

Behind us, Kheppy had reclaimed the front windowsill, safely out of Pickles's reach, which was wise, considering the pug seemed thoroughly enamored with her.

I maneuvered Claire to a seat near Delphine, the farthest possible point from Merle without making it obvious. I wasn't jealous. Just territorial. It had been a week.

As everyone settled, I realized we didn't have anything to drink on the table, so I slipped into the kitchen to grab something from the refrigerator. When I saw the lemonade in the pitcher, my heart almost stopped.

Sorry, Delphine. No way was I bringing that memory to our feast. I dumped it into the sink and reached for the iced tea mix instead.

When I walked back into the dining room with the pitcher, the air hummed with cheerful, overlapping voices.

I set the tea on the table and slipped into my seat.

For the first time since Evangeline collapsed in my backyard, the house was full.

And it felt safe.

Not perfect. We were too bruised for that.

But good.

I let my gaze drift around the table, taking them in one by one—Delphine's fierce, unwavering love. Willa's tender, hard-won courage. Opal's steady calm. Merle's open, unguarded heart. Howard's quiet readiness to step in wherever he was needed. Claire's warmth and easy cheer. And Lila and Luna, finally in the same room.

And, of course, Kheppy.

My constant companion. My forever friend.

Something settled inside me.

Not triumph. Not quite relief.

But optimism.

Whatever came of the werewolves' petition with the High Council was a problem for another day.

If they regained their council seat, we'd adjust. We always did.

And if the Duval estate tried to tug Lila back into old obligations and older guilt, it would have me to deal with.

I wouldn't run from a fight. Not anymore.

Tomorrow there would be a difficult goodbye, but today, we had this moment.

Kheppy lifted her silver-gray head, amber eyes catching the candlelight. She regarded the room with the gravity of a cat who'd seen empires rise and fall, then she hopped down from her windowsill perch and made her way to my lap.

"You have survived," she said. Not to the room, but to me.

It wasn't praise. Just recognition.

Then she curled into a ball and settled. Her purr rumbled against me like a quiet benediction.

"Yes, I have," I whispered back and smiled before reaching for the stuffing Delphine was handing me to pass along to Merle.

Now, we had a feast. And laughter. And the quiet certainty that whatever came next, we'd face it together.

Boo and Kheppy's sleuthing adventures will continue in the Laguna Bay Midlife Witch Cozy Mystery series. Learn more at https://DeAnnaDrake.com.

Free Novella (Subscriber Exclusive)

GRAB *DEAD END DATE*, a free novella available exclusively to members of my Cozy Mystery Readers Club. The book is part of the Purr-fect Relic series, which is where Boo and Kheppy first made their debut. Within its pages, you'll discover how Rebecca and Kheppy's sister, Aneksi, hunt down a killer during Rebecca's first date with Detective Nick Devon at Citrus Grove's hottest new nightspot. *Dead End Date* can be read as a stand-alone story, but it fits chronologically between *Paws, Claws, and Curses* and *Hisses, Hexes, and Homicide*.

When you join me and other cozy mystery readers in the Cozy Mystery Readers Club, you'll also have access to free puzzles, book-related recipes, behind-the-scenes tidbits, and other bonus content. Sign up at DeAnnaDrake.com/join. It's free and easy, and you won't miss any of the fun!

Dear Reader

THANK YOU SO MUCH for taking the time to read *Moonlight, Magic, and Murder*, the third book in the Laguna Bay Midlife Witch Cozy Mystery series. It's been such a joy to share the adventures—and occasional misadventures—of these Laguna Bay characters, who have truly captured my heart and found their place in the Magical Cats universe alongside the Citrus Grove crew from the Purr-fect Relic Cozy Mysteries.

If you've enjoyed spending time with Boo, Kheppy, and the rest of the gang, I'd be so grateful if you'd consider leaving a short review at your favorite retailer or review site. Even a few words can make a big difference in helping other readers discover the series—and it means more to me than you know.

Bonus Recipe: DELPHINE'S APPLE STRUDEL MUFFINS

DELPHINE'S APPLE STRUDEL MUFFINS

These are the kind of muffins that fill the house with cinnamon and comfort—the kind that make everything feel a little cozier and brighter, and make you want to brew up a pot of tea and curl up with your favorite mystery.

Yield: About 12 muffins | Prep Time: 20–25 minutes | Bake Time: 18–22 minutes

Ingredients:

Muffin Batter

2 cups all-purpose flour

1 cup granulated sugar
1/2 cup brown sugar, packed
2 tsp baking powder
1/2 tsp baking soda
1/2 tsp salt
2 tsp cinnamon
1/2 tsp nutmeg
1/2 cup unsalted butter, melted
2 large eggs
3/4 cup milk (or buttermilk for extra richness)
2 tsp vanilla extract
2 cups apples, peeled and diced (Honeycrisp or Granny Smith)

Cinnamon Sugar Filling (Strudel Swirl)

1/3 cup brown sugar
1 1/2 tsp cinnamon
1 tbsp melted butter

Streusel Topping

1/2 cup flour
1/3 cup brown sugar
1 tsp cinnamon
1/4 cup cold butter, cubed

Optional Vanilla Glaze

3/4 cup powdered sugar
1–2 tbsp milk
1/2 tsp vanilla

Instructions:

Make the Streusel by mixing the flour, brown sugar, and cinnamon. Cut in the cold butter until crumbly. Set aside.

Make the Batter, by whisking together in one bowl the flour, sugars, baking powder, baking soda, salt, cinnamon, and nutmeg. In another bowl, whisk together the melted butter, eggs, milk, and vanilla. Combine the wet and dry ingredients just until mixed. Fold in the diced apples.

To create the layered strudel effect, fill the muffin cups halfway. Add a spoonful of the cinnamon sugar filling, then top with more batter. Sprinkle generously with streusel.

Bake 18–22 minutes, until the tops are golden and a toothpick comes out clean.

Drizzle the glaze (optional but recommended) over the muffins after they have cooled slightly.

Delphine's Tips:

- For deeper flavor, sauté the apples briefly in butter and cinnamon before adding them to the batter. It will bring out their sweetness in the loveliest way.

- If you're serving these with tea, I'd reach for a honeyed chamomile for something soft and soothing. But if you're in the mood for something a little brighter, a classic black tea like Earl Grey pairs beautifully with the apples.

- For those bakery-style tops, fill the muffin cups just a touch higher and don't be shy with the streusel.

A Recipe Note from Delphine:

I'll be the first to admit—this isn't one of my usual vegan bakes. But every now and then, especially this time of year, I believe in making room for a little indulgence. And these apple strudel muffins? They're worth it.

They're warm with cinnamon, sweet with apples, and just rich enough to feel like a proper treat shared in good company. I like to think recipes like this aren't about perfection—they're about comfort, connection, and those quiet moments in the kitchen when everything smells like home.

Bake them for someone you love, and don't forget to save one for yourself.

Books by DeAnna Drake and the Author's Other Work

LAGUNA BAY MIDLIFE WITCH COZY MYSTERY SERIES

Candy, Cauldrons, and a Corpse
Ghosts, Lies, and Alibis
Moonlight, Magic, and Murder

MAGICAL CATS COZY MYSTERY SERIES

Trouble at the Christmas Tea (novella)
Lady Paws and the Christmas Caper (short story)

A PURR-FECT RELIC COZY MYSTERY SERIES

Paws, Claws, and Curses
Dead End Date (novella)
Hisses, Hexes, and Homicide
Furballs and Felonies

Crime and Cat-astrophes
Blackmail and Kitty Tails
Whiskers and Ciphers

A MAGICAL MOUSE CAPER SERIES

Mouse in the House

FANTASY FICTION WRITTEN AS D.D. CROIX

THE QUEEN'S FAYTE SERIES

Memory Thief (prequel story)
Dragonfly Maid
Slivering Curse
Shadow Rite
Guardian of the Realm

HISTORICAL AND CONTEMPORARY ROMANCE WRITTEN AS DEANNA CAMERON

THE DANCER CHRONICLES

The Girl on the Midway Stage
The Girl on the Vaudeville Stage

CALIFORNIA BELLY DANCE ROMANCE SERIES

Shimmy for Me
Dance with Me
Jingly Bells

About DeAnna Drake

DeAnna Drake writes warm, witty, magical cozy mysteries filled with heart, humor, and unforgettable feline companions.

Her books blend the charm of small-town cozies with the depth of character-driven fantasy—where ancient magic lingers, secrets refuse to stay buried, and talking cats with centuries of history always seem to know more than they're saying.

DeAnna is the author of the *Purr-fect Relic Cozy Mystery* series and the *Laguna Bay Midlife Witch Cozy Mysteries*, two interconnected worlds tied together by long-lived magical cats, cursed relics, supernatural politics, and found-family bonds. Readers love her stories for their emotional resonance, rich world-building, relatable midlife heroines, and the blend of mystery, magic, and heart.

If you enjoy cozy escapes with layered characters, gentle humor, twisty mysteries, and a touch of ancient wonder, you'll feel right at home in the Magical Cats Universe.

Under different names, DeAnna writes young-adult fantasy fiction, contemporary romances, and historical novels set in the Victorian and Edwardian eras.

When she isn't plotting new adventures for her characters, she enjoys afternoon tea, binging crime shows, and escaping to Disneyland whenever she can.

She lives in Southern California with her family, which includes her two favorite people and one ridiculously pampered border collie. Learn more at https://DeAnnaDrake.com.

Facebook:
https://www.facebook.com/DeAnnaDrakeWrites
Instagram:
https://www.instagram.com/DeAnnaDrakeAuthor

www.ingramcontent.com/pod-product-compliance
Lightning Source LLC
LaVergne TN
LVHW091120080826
845145LV00008B/1989

* 9 7 8 1 9 5 7 6 9 1 0 5 3 *